MW00936714

Run to My River

by

Yvonne Dorsey

Run to My River
Copyright 2008 Yvonne Dorsey
ISBN: 1 4196-5199-4
ISBN-13   978-1 4196-5199-1
Library of Congress Control Number 2006909486

Run to My River

Run to My River and its fictional ancestral book "**Powhantuwa's River**" are precursors to the final fictional story in **Section Two of this book.**

The final story in section two, "**The Haunting of Shannon Fitzpatrick.**" on the same river, was set in motion centuries before she was born, on a river she loved.

The Choptank River, on the eastern shore of Maryland, was once the home of a First Native American Tribe, The Choptanks. Their lives, and then their spirits, wove in and out of each other's existence, until one desperate spirit managed to communicate with the millennial, **Shannon Fitzpatrick**.

This book is written in two sections:

The first:
The Life of Shaahatuck on her river

The second:
The Life of Shannon on the same river

Although they lived in starkly different times, centuries apart, **Shannon** and the Ancient, **Shaahatuck**, managed to forge an incredibly fearful, yet empathetic relationship and helped each other through difficult times

Credits

Story and Poetry	Yvonne Dorsey
Sharing her Eastern Shore	Marie Rush Beck
Photography for Book Cover Choptank River, Maryland	Yvonne Dorsey
Photography for Book Cover High Bridge, New Jersey	Rose Ranauro

Cover Models:

Native American Ghost	Renee' Yvonne Ketterer
Model's Photographer	Marie Rush Beck
Modern Woman	Kimberly Helen Pickell
Model's Photographer	Rose Dorsey Ranauro
Cover Design First American Cross	Keith David Ketterer Kimberly Helen Pickell

I have used italics throughout the book to separate a thought from the current reading, to share memories told by a character, or to insert some bits of information.

Poetry is also in italics because I am a romantic. Sometimes, I think italics add a sense of emotion to poetry – Yvonne

Acknowledgements

I thank my special readers for their insightful comments and suggestions for this 2015 book:

Susan Hayes

Mary Kay Mitchell

Buck Boccansuso

Anne Walters

Keith Ketterer

John Perry

Rose Ranauro

Eleanor Irons

Marjorie Goble

Jim Fealey

Kimberly Pickell

Corey Ranauro

Katherine Bagin Theleman

Marilyn Stowell

Wallace Dorsey Sr.

No person mentioned above received monetary compensation for reading and/or commenting on the pre-published transcript of this book.

Pleading Eyes

The young girl ran alongside the car. Her frantic, wild, dark, pleading eyes were staring through the side window at Shannon Fitzpatrick.

"OH my Go..." Shannon cried aloud.

Ian, Shannon's husband, startled by her outcry, turned abruptly to her and demanded, "Shannon, what's wrong? What's wrong? Are you all right. Luv?"

Shannon could only say, "She's out there! She's out there!" Ian impatiently asked, "Who, what's out there?"

Shannon looked again at the window and only saw a lone tree in the middle of a field of golden leaves and lots and lots of blue sky. However, she was positive she saw a young girl running alongside the automobile, but staring through the window at the same time, obviously pleading for help.

Shannon held her breath for a second and tried to understand the frightening and yet very sad occurrence. Trying to collect her thought, she was positive she saw someone, possibly a young girl wearing an ancient garment. She could not make any sense of it. It happened so quickly, and then it was over, but she was certain something mystical did happen to her.

One minute, she was riding along, drinking in the blissful morning October sunshine, in conversation with the man she adored. The next minute, she was staring into dark scared eyes, staring back at her. A sadness encompassing her was so severe that it brought her almost to the point of tears. Her heart was pounding. Fear soon replaced her sadness. As suddenly as it began, it was over. The vision lasted only for a moment. To Shannon, it would be a lasting experience, and her life would never be the same because of it.

Section One

CENTURIES EARLIER

The Story of Shaahatuck
On Her River

Yvonne Dorsey

Preface

An excruciating pain shot through the belly of Shaahatuck (shh-ha-tuck). She thought an arrow had pierced her. So sure she was under enemy attack, she tried to crawl behind a giant tree for safety, falling to the ground. Her body was in agony; blood was spilling out of her onto the ground. Suddenly, she realized an enemy arrow had not pierced her, but that she was losing her baby. The only remaining evidence of her life and love was literally exploding and leaving her body.

In emotional and physical pain, she buried her face in the dirt and fallen leaves. All alone in the forest, her young body suffered childbirth. Her soul was forlorn. Fluids from her eyes and mouth began creating mud under her face. She sobbed, "Our baby is with you; I want to be with you." She felt dirty and forgotten by the Father Spirit. She was extremely weak and saddened by her miscarriage. However, she knew she had to purify her baby's remains.

She created a fire, using a small pile of leaves and twigs, over her baby's remains. She put out the fire, let it smoke for a few minutes, and then quickly used a large twig to spread the ashes so they would cool quickly. Gathering the tiny bit of her baby's remains, she wrapped them in more leaves and mud made by her own tears and moist fertile earth.

Suddenly realizing the smell of new birth on her body and clothing would quickly attract animals, Shaahatuck panicked. She cried, "What have I done? What have I done? I must hurry. She cried aloud, "Help me. Help me, Great Spirit. Please help me!" She ran with her precious package, crying, "The Father Spirit will bless you my little one. He will take you to Manassaquoit (man-a-squa)." She headed for her place of solace, the river.

Memories of her life, past joys and excruciating wretchedness that brought her to that day, haunted her as she ran.

Yvonne Dorsey

CHAPTER ONE
Memories
Shaahatuck and Manassaquoit
Their Beginning

Manassaquoit, son of **Chief Manakouk** and his mate, **Hatsawa**, was taller than most men in his tribe. He was very handsome and accomplished at every chosen endeavor. Many young girls in the tribe aspired to be his mate.

Shaahatuck was the **daughter** of **Powhantuwa** and the chief's younger brother, **Wamquwa**. She was the grandniece of **Hoquai**, her mother's sister. Even when she was young, the face of Manassaquoit was always in her dreams. She prayed often that she would someday be his mate.

In Shaahatuck's twelfth year, her mother, Powhantuwa, began feeling weak, not sick, just weak. Though she was eating, she seemed to be lacking the nutrition her body needed to build life-sustaining blood. The Healing Elder ordered special broth to develop nutrition in her body, but nothing helped. As the days passed into months, she became weaker.

Powhantuwa knew her time with her precious daughter was nearing the end. One day, struggling to walk, she took Shaahatuck by the hand. They went to the tent of Manakouk and Hatsawa. She said to them, "In a few days, my spirit will be with Wamquwa. Hoquia will keep Shaahatuck in her wigwam for her sleep, but Hoquia is older and I do not want to burden her with the total care of my daughter. I want to give you my Shaahatuck to be your child. Will you accept her?"

Hatsawa wanted to say words to the contrary that her dear sister-in-law would soon recover, but she knew in her heart that Powhantuwa could not be healed and would soon be with the spirits.

Young Shaahatuck stood silent as she listened to her elders.

1

Suddenly, she lashed out at her mother, saying, "No, no, you cannot go to Wamquwa. You must stay with me." She repeated as she ran from the wigwam, "You must stay with me." She could not comprehend the thought of her mother having no control of her own circumstance.

Later that night Powhantuwa tried to console her daughter. Young Shaahatuck would not discuss her mother's illness. Powhantuwa was too weak to continue the conversation. She collapsed and passed out. Shaahatuck lay on her chest and cried herself to sleep.

The next morning, while Hatsawa was tending to the needs of Powhantuwa, Chief Manakouk asked Shaahatuck to sit with him for the morning meal. Shaahatuck obliged. Manakouk handed her a piece of bread. She took it and began eating. He said to her, "Shaahatuck, do you taste the good grains?" Shaahatuck nodded. He handed her a bowl of cornmeal mush. She accepted the bowl and began soaking her bread in the mush. As she ate the soggy bread, Manakouk continued, "Shaahatuck, do you know that the food we eat gives us life?"

Shaahatuck answered, "I do not know. I just know we eat and we live."

Chief Manakouk said, "Yes, we live because our bodies use the food we eat to help us grow strong. Sometimes, our bodies become sick and cannot use the food we eat. We can do nothing about it. We are not to blame for the way natures treats us." Shaahatuck looked at the chief, trying to comprehend his words.

The chief continued, "Do you not know your mother cannot heal her own body? Her body is in control. She cannot stay with us. Can you not be angry with her? Can you let her go in peace to my brother, your father, Wamquwa?"

Shaahatuck cried and was ashamed of her behavior. She spilled her mush as she threw herself into her uncle's arms. After a few moments, she stood, said, "I want to go to her."

Manakouk whispered, "Be gentle with your mother." Shaahatuck wiped her tears and nodded. She went to her mother's bed, snuggled in her arms and cried herself to sleep.

The next day, Powhantuwa asked Manakouk to take her to the river, to the Prayer Rock. Manakouk asked her if she wanted to be alone. She declined, saying that she wanted the tribe to be with her. They had accepted her, when she was an orphaned Powhantuwa baby. She became a vital member of the Choptank Tribe.

The Choptank Tribe called a group of rocks the Mighty Prayer Rock, because they were so close together they resembled a very large rock. They often referred to it as the Prayer Rock or The Praying Rock. The largest of the piled up rocks loomed over the rest, and seemed to resemble a giant bird's wing preparing to soar to the sky. The tribe truly believed the Father Spirit designed the prayer rock as their sanctuary. Powhantuwa's mother died there after she safely brought Powhantuwa to the Choptank Village. It was a very special to the tribe of the Choptank.

One by one the people gathered and bade a sad farewell to the young woman they adopted several years before. She asked them to chant and dance. As they did, she smiled, closed her eyes and went to her eternal sleep.

Manassaquoit and Tucahaunna stood by Shaahatuck. Tucahaunna said, "Today, you are our sister."

Manassaquoit echoed his statement, "We will always be your family. You are not alone."

After the death of her mother, Shaahatuck depended on her great aunt, Hoquia, sister of Running Doe, the adopted mother of Powhantuwa. Shaahatuck also depended on Manakouk and Hatsawa to be her teachers. She slept in the tent of Hoquia.

Hoquia was a strong support for Powhantuwa, just as she had been to Running Doe and Powhantuwa. When she was of an advanced age, she developed a serious lung disease, and died shortly before Shaahatuck's Ceremonial Womanhood Run. Her death created a void in the lives of the tribe. Shaahatuck became more and more dependent on Hatsawa for guidance, and lived for the day she and Manassaquoit would create a large family. However, before he could even consider choosing a mate, Manassaquoit had to prove his manhood. When he became of age, he went on his Vision Quest, (proving time) which was the custom for all young boys at a certain age. Their success, alone in the wilderness, without any food, weapons, or creature comforts, demonstrated their manhood. They had to meet and conquer all obstacles nature hurled at them and were very responsible for their own survival.

Manassaquoit spent one week alone in the wilderness, proving his manhood. He spent time in meditation, praying to the Father Spirit for guidance. Once his manhood, and his right to be the future chief of the Choptank, was established, he was allowed by the chief of the tribe to elect a mate to bear his children.

Shaahatuck feared that when Manassaquoit returned from the wilderness, he would choose some other young woman for a mate. She was suspicious of every young girl who looked at him. She vowed she would lure him away from all suitors. She prayed to the Father Spirit to allow her to become the mate of the magnificent Choptank brave.

Manassaquoit only had eyes for Shaahatuck. He admired her beauty and loved her spirit. Her hair was so black and shiny it looked dark blue. He loved that she was shorter than most girls of the tribe. He loved her as a child, and every day since. He was proud and happy to be living along the Choptank River. He wanted to live and grow old right there with her. When he did return, Shaahatuck quickly learned that she had no reason to worry. Once she said to him,

"I loved you as I was coming out of my mother's body. You must have been playing very near my parent's wigwam, just waiting for my appearance into the world."

Manassaquoit laughed, picked her up in his strong arms, and whirled her around. They loved their time together: fishing, hunting, playing or just sitting along the Choptank River. They made their marks on the Prayer Rock many times: once when they were little children, and then later when they were teens. They visited the rock often. Their intense friendship grew into a deep love. They were truly happy together.

When Manassaquoit announced to the tribe that he chose Shaahatuck for his future mate, his mother, Hatsawa was very happy. The season of the full moon was chosen for their joining. However, shortly before that day, Hatsawa died of a simple wound she received when a thorn pricked her ankle as she was picking berries. The ankle became diseased very quickly. Even the respected Healing Elder could not save her. She died in the arms of Manakouk, begging him to protect her sons from harm. He promised to devout his life to their sons and the tribe.

Manakouk mourned the death of Hatsawa, and vowed never to have another mate.

During the season of the full moon, Manassaquoit and Shaahatuck stood side by side in a Flower Circle, on a bed of sand and autumn leaves, near the Prayer Rock. Chief Manakouk chanted to the Father Spirit on their behalf and pronounced they were one. Shaahatuck's dream had come true. She was body and soul, one with Manassaquoit. The all night celebration went on much too long for her. For as long as she could remember, she had dreamed of making love with him. Her dream finally came true; it was a magical night. She was truly in love and totally his.

For almost five years, the young couple enjoyed their married life along the Choptank River. However, in those years together, Shaahatuck had not given her husband a child. She felt that the Father Spirit had not smiled upon her. She prayed always for forgiveness, feeling she was barren because she must have done something offensive. She reasoned it must be her fault. Her husband was the future chief. He needed to have a son to carry on his authority.

Chief Manakouk loved Shaahatuck as a daughter, but often wondered if the marriage was a mistake. She appeared to be barren. However, when he watched the young couple, he thought of how he loved his own woman when they were young, and how he still loved her spirit. He knew Manassaquoit and Shaahatuck had the same love. He made the 'wait and see' decision. He would often sigh "What will be, will be." He resigned himself to his belief that the Father Spirit would provide all needs.

Although Shaahatuck was gloriously happy to be the mate of Manassaquoit, the lack of pregnancy, combined with the mourning of all of her mother figures, was causing her to become despondent. When Manassaquoit realized how lonely she was when he went out hunting or fishing, he pleaded with his father to allow her to accompany the hunting parties. The chief reminded Manassaquoit that it was not usual, but finally agreed to the request on a trial basis.

Manakouk's decision angered some of the other women, but they knew of Shaahatuck's unhappy, empty heart, with no child to hold. They eventually adapted to Manakouk's decision. They felt it was better than having her mope around all day, worthless in her grief. At least they would eat. She was a very good hunter and every bit as capable with a bow and a fishing spear as the tribesmen. She often caught more fish than many of them, which help provide dinner for the entire tribe. Considering the situation, Chief Manakouk's final decision boiled down to the hope of Shaahatuck possibly getting pregnant while they were out in the wilderness, away from the pressure of the daily tribal duties.

In addition to hunting, fishing and trapping, Shaahatuck was also very accomplished at all the chores expected of a young woman. When she became a mother, she would certainly be prepared. Until then, she was content to be with Manassaquoit, to have him as her mate, to hunt and fish in their peaceful Choptank region. One day that peace was threatened.

CHAPTER TWO
Run to the Village

While the parties were on a hunting and fishing expedition, messengers ran through the forest and along the river sounding alarms, summoning all hunting and fishing parties, which included Shaahatuck, to return to camp.

Runners, carrying bows and arrows, charged past Shaahatuck. While attempting to run at a faster pace, she stumbled and fell into a bed of rocks along the path. Her head felt as if it would explode; her mouth was burning, her elbows saturated with blood and gravel. She struggled to fight feminine tears. When Manassaquoit held out his hand to help her stand, her ankle gave way to extreme pain. Realizing that it was probably broken, she motioned for him to go ahead without her.

Manassaquoit nodded in agreement. He left one of the younger hunters to help her, and then resumed his powerful run back to their village. As the chief's son and aide, he needed to be by his father's side.

The young hunter gathered vines and branches to wrap Shaahatuck's ankle and selected a strong tree limb for her to use as a crutch. They continued through the forest toward the river.

Shaahatuck, becoming more and angry with each agonizing hobble, and having concern for the immediate summons back to the village, shouted, "What is wrong? What is wrong?" Her startled young escort said nothing, but he knew that the abrupt call to the encampment was obviously serious. Possible scenarios crept in and out of Shaahatuck's mind. The worst of which was that her beloved Chief Manakouk (Man-uh-coke) had died.

Knowing that voicing her distress was using precious air and energy, she resolved to keep quiet and concentrate on getting back to the village as quickly as possible. She painfully continued her journey back to the village. When they finally entered the compound, she saw Manassaquoit and his younger brother, Tucahaunna (talk-uh-haunna), speaking with the chief. Their reaction to his words appeared serious. She was relieved that Manakouk was ok. Still, she was concerned.

The three men, leaders of the tribe, walked away from the crowd to continue their conversation. Shaahatuck joined the others. She knew that Chief Manakouk would relate the situation when he was ready.

As they prepared the evening meal, several people whispered a rumor that a cruel tribe had been seen on the peninsula. Though the villagers attempted to work as usual, they were shrouded in fear.

Shaahatuck was distracted from her duties. In her lifetime, no tribe had attempted a conquest of their territory. However, she remembered hearing her father, crying about the 'Cruel Devils.' She also remembered her mother trying to calm him. Shaahatuck had been spared details of past invasions, so she had no way of knowing they were real, or that her precious region could become the home of a hostile, aggressive tribe.

The tribesmen shared in the responsibility of being on constant watch for enemy invaders. The young men took their turn at strategic lookout posts at many locations surrounding their encampment. This was not a volunteer position, but a part of a mandatory, very organized operation. It was a part of their daily life. If a tribesman was not on sentry duty, he was working for the tribe: hunting, fishing and trapping. The tribe did not wish for war, had never been involved in one during Shaahatuck's lifetime, but they were prepared for it.

The tribe took time for prayers, relaxing conversation, and a lot of play, but spent much of their time working for their survival, the protection of the tribe, and preservation of their precious homeland.

Everyone shared in the responsibilities. The women maintained an adequate supply of dried foods. There was always enough to carry with them should they have to make a sudden move. The men made weapons. Overall, life was still very good along the Choptank River. However, that day was not a very tranquil one. Eventually, villagers would learn, that sentinels, part of an eight-man team on watch far north of their encampment, had discovered a small, seemingly temporary camp of the *Shanaquoix* (Shua-nock-qua), a Western Shore Tribe. Though the Shanaquoix did inhabit the Western Shore, and usually stayed on their land, the threat of an attack was always in the mind of elders of the Eastern Shore Tribes.

The sentinels had reported that there were no women, children, old people or animals in the Shanaquoix encampment. There were only very strong looking men and their horses. To the sentinels, it appeared to be a gathering of a war party from across the Big Water, preparing to come down river to attack the peaceful villages, attempting an invasion of the entire peninsula.

The Shanaquoix, unaware of their observers, were relaxing and eating, obviously preparing themselves for battle. Chief Manakouk assumed they had a new chief. He reasoned the new chief must have decided to break the pact the old one had declared, and was attempting to take over the peninsula, even southeast to the Great Waters (Atlantic Ocean).

After hearing the sentinels report, Chief Manakouk assumed they were probably waiting for more of their tribe to join them, gaining strength in numbers to be stronger for battle. Per previous arrangements, he dispatched messengers to notify the other tribes on their peninsula. He knew the tribes would quickly prepare themselves, and join the Choptank in defending the territory.

Chief Manakouk knew getting to the Shanaquoix camp before they began their invasion would be impossible. He also knew the established, protective Alliance must join forces and fight the Shanaquoix. Many braves assembled and prepared themselves for battle.

Chief Manakouk instructed the tribe to go deep into the forest to a pre-selected area and await the return of the protectors. Patrols went into the forest and up river to stand guard while the remaining defenders prepared to leave camp. The tribe packed only what they needed for temporary evacuation. To preserve their remaining supplies, they dug holes and tightly wrapped all the root vegetables they could do without for a while. They buried them deep in the ground, covering the food graves with dried straw and stones to hide them from the animals.

As Shaahatuck methodically worked, she thought, "I'm sure many tribes want our land. Today feels different somehow. Maybe it is because I am now older. I know more things. I know the chances of losing…"

Though her fears brought instant pain to her heart, and her ankle continued to swell, Shaahatuck kept to her tasks, knowing the security of the tribe came before everything else. However, she had a secret she had planned to share with Manassaquoit that night. It saddened her that she would not be alone with him before he left the village. She thought about the child he had been awaiting, possibly a son who just might be on his way to their arms. She was sure the Father Spirit would honor her with a boy-child she could present to her mate. It would be her reward for her patience and continued prayers. It was to be a joyous night, but she dared not distract Manassaquoit. She vowed to keep her secret in her heart and wait for his return. Choking back tears, she worked harder than she really wanted. She wished she could grab Manassaquoit. The two of them would run, disappear into the forest and live all alone. She desperately needed him to stay with her, but she knew she had to let him go. Manassaquoit promised to meet with her before he left. He sat in the wigwam with his brother and father, discussing strategy. They ate only enough food for strength and then rested only long enough to be refreshed.

The religious leader of the tribe stood outside the tent, praying for their safety and success in battle.

Shaahatuck went to the river to bathe. She wanted the clean scent of her body to remain in the heart of Manassaquoit. Knowing she would have only a few precious moments with him, she hurriedly walked out of the river. Manassaquoit watched her as she put on her garment, and then held out his arms. She grabbed his big hand and pleaded, "Manassaquoit, please come back to me." They walked along the river, side by side, and headed back to camp.

Manassaquoit hated to go. He certainly hated the idea of war. He hated leaving his lover, his life-mate, especially with her in so much physical and emotional pain. He wished they had a child, maybe a son who would give her comfort in his absence, and possibly take care of her should he not return. For a short time, he had suspected there might be one on the way. Shaahatuck did not mention one; he had dismissed the thought.

The young couple stopped walking and stood alongside the river they loved. The sand warmed their feet. The sound of the splashing water reflected their love. Manassaquoit turned to Shaahatuck, took her shoulders in his strong hands and, trying to reassure her, said, "Shaahatuck, I have always loved you. I will come back to you. We will live long lives. You will be sick of the sight of me, and will always be complaining to our children about what a pest I am to you. We will grow old and go to the Father Spirit as old ones, together." He kissed her tenderly, long, lovingly and then hard. He could not bear to let her go. He longed for the warmth and comfort of her body. He desperately needed to make passionate love to her, and to carry her love with him, but it would be a very definite distraction. The fact that it was a rule of war meant nothing. They needed their love. The rushing of footsteps brought them to reality. It was time to leave.

Manassaquoit gently dropped his hands from Shaahatuck's trembling shoulders, held onto her hands for a moment while touching his forehead to hers, turned and walked away. She stood motionless as she watched him join the other defenders.

In the span of only a few minutes, the men painted their bodies and gathered their weapons. The hunter/fishermen turned warriors were on their horses in formation, and ready for war. Warriors were on each side of the front line. Chief Manakouk and his two sons were in the middle.

Chief Manakouk reminded the young men, who were assigned to guard the tribe, to wait in the forest until the "All Clear" was sounded. He nodded, "Onward." Manassaquoit gave a loud signal. They rode off. The sound of the words "All Clear," gave some hope to Shaahatuck. As she watched the formation disappear, she thought, "Yes, they will be back victorious." Reassuringly, she whispered, "He will come back to me. Why do I grieve the Father Spirit?" She busied herself with the task of helping the little ones prepare for the long walk into the forest.

The tribe loaded supplies on the backs of horses and were very quickly settled in their temporary home in the forest. In their new home, near a flowing stream, women were grinding grain, babies were crying, and children were playing. As a precaution, young men, working in shifts, were stationed around the perimeter of the new camp. Older women were weaving. Older men were shaving sticks into weapons. Life went on as it always had.

As Shaahatuck looked around the camp, she thought, "Nothing has changed for them. Do they not feel? Do they not care? Have they no heart?" She knew better, and was allowing her fear to control her logic. Reprimanding herself, she said, "Of course they care." She knew they cried in their hearts for their mate, their brother, their sons. Reprimanding herself, she said, "Who am I to judge?" She felt ashamed and pledged to do her part. She would work and pray for sleep. She vowed to wait as bravely as the others and join in their evening prayers for the safe return of their men.

As she watched the methodical activities around the camp, Shaahatuck felt more alone than ever. She had no children to comfort her, nor a mother's shoulder on which to shed her tears. As she fought depression, she asked, "Why must my special people die and leave me? Have I not pleased the Father Spirit? Will he also take away my Manassaquoit to punish me for my sins?" She wrapped her arms around her middle, wishing she had told him about the baby before he left, but they had waited so long. She wanted the night she told him to be a wonderful, happy time, when they would celebrate the spirit within her, the little one destined to grow up and be a great chief of their nation.

As the day turned to dusk, Shaahatuck watched the other women tend to their children. She cried inwardly, "Only one sun, and now the moon is rising without Manassaquoit! Not even one more sun can I take! Not one more sun!" She felt the forest closing in on her. She needed to be in the open air, near the water. She needed to go into the water. She also needed to pray to the Father Spirit to cleanse her of any sins she might have committed, and she needed to be alone to pray. The urge to run was overwhelming. She knew what she had to do.

When the village was quiet and everyone was, hopefully, asleep, she packed her belongings in her bedroll, and put a small amount of food in her backpack. At the first light, and knowing that she was courting danger of wild animals, she prepared to leave the camp. After a guard walked past her, she quickly ran away from the forest toward the river. When she approached the clearing that gave view to the water she whispered, "Oh Father Spirit, the sight of the river thrills me. Please give me peace."

Crushing autumn leaves, she raced through the field toward the river. Instantly, she felt spiritually closer to Manassaquoit. She quickly made a hiding place on the riverside of the giant rock. Using a small log as a tool, she dug a cave in the sand. Hoping to make it look it like the remains of a dead tree, she surrounded it with tree limbs, twigs, branches and leaves. When she was finished, she took the chance of going back to the clearing and looked at her creation. Being satisfied that she had substantially hidden her new abode, and comforted by the familiar surroundings, she thought, "This is good. Here, I can have my face washed with the mist from the river. Here, I will pray to the Father Spirit while I wait."

Reminding herself of the danger of standing out in the open, she quickly returned to her cave and peered out across the water. The view from her new abode was sedative. The sight of the river always made her feel so alive, so loved and so welcome. It was her home. That day it was her refuge and comfort. She ate and rested from her journey out of the forest and her laborious tasks.

At high noon, when the day was the warmest, Shaahatuck took off her garment and stepped into the water. Being sure to stay out of sight of anyone approaching from the west, she stood in the water and prayed. She stayed in the water for only a few minutes, and then immersed herself for a final cleansing; she stepped out onto the sand, dried herself with the warm sun, dressed and then slept most of the afternoon, in her 'cave'. When she awoke, she sat in prayer. She knew she would have to pray quietly.

Prayers were usually wonderful, loud, beautiful chants, so the Father Spirit would hear them and grant blessings. Shaahatuck wondered how she could pray so quietly. However, she faced the east and raised her arms in reverence. She begged for mercy for her people, especially for her Manassaquoit. For the rest of the day she sat in quiet meditation, seldom ate, hardly slept.

As she sat out as far as she dared in the warm noonday sun, tears swelled in her eyes. She remembered her mother, Powhantuwa; she was sitting in the same area of the river where her mother sat during her last hours, on the day she died.

She sighed and remembered her mother, Powhantuwa, telling her stories. She especially enjoyed the one about her father, Wamquwa.

Powhantuwa said,

"When I became a woman, Wamquwa took me for his mate. He was so happy when I told him you were in my belly. You knew just when to enter the world. You were born on the very

day that your grandfather's spirit went to the clouds. Your birth gave your father comfort during the grief of his own father. Wamquwa was dancing, chanting prayers for the spirit of his father. When I started my labor, he turned his prayers to the Father Spirit on my behalf, and for you, our little Shaahatuck."

Shaahatuck smiled at her bittersweet memories. She sat quietly enjoying the river, trying to keep positive about Manassaquoit's safe return. She reminisced about the day she became his mate.

She thought, "It was a day just like today." She threw herself back in the sand and looked up to the sky. She happily mocked her remembrance, "These leaves fall soft upon my face as they did that day many suns ago." On the morning of their joining, she had lain in the sand, and raised her hands up to the heavens and sighed, "What a good day." She thought of the fact that she loved standing in his shadow when the sun was at his back. Because of the bright sunlight shining in her eyes, she only saw his sexual, shadowy image. This always put her in a dream state, creating an erotic aura that thrilled her soul.

Shaahatuck smiled as she touched the string of the tiny bits of shell called Roanoke and played with the string of clam and mussel shells called Wampum-Peak. Manassaquoit had placed them around her neck: the Roanoke on the day Chief Manakouk gave his blessing on their union and the Wampum-Peak on the day they became one spirit. Those shells were valuable and used for monetary trading, so she felt blessed. She remembered the wonderful dream come true morning before their joining, she sat on the bank of the river and chanted,

"Oh Father Spirit in the Clouds, please give me much happiness with Manassaquoit. Please tell him to love me as I love him and give us many, many children to bless our old age.

15

Please let us live a long happy life, and then beckon us to come to you as old ones, together."

As she rested, she remembered that as she spoke those words, she let the sand sift through her fingers, counting "one, two, three, four…" giggling at the prospect of motherhood. In sweet remembrance of that happy day, she did the same, counting, "one, two, three, four…" She sighed and repeated, "It was a very good day."

Exhausted and being bathed in the warmth of the beautiful autumn sun, she closed her eyes and out of habit before falling asleep, she prayed.

" Great Spirit in the Clouds "

Thank you for all things.
Please give me peace in my sleep.
Let me awake in your love,
and then, smile on me
In your beautiful sunshine.

She fell into a deep sleep and had a dream. In it,

She was walking on a snow-covered field. Off in the distance she saw a figure coming toward her. The figure fell. She tried to run to it. She could not move forward; her feet were frozen in the snow. She knelt, and cupping her hands, she gathered the snow. The snow turned to burning flames, and then to ashes which began to smoke. The ashes scorched her hands. She let them slip through her fingers. Gray streams of wind and ash fell to the ground and became snow again.

She screamed as she awoke, "Ohha. Ohha. Ohha." She felt as if a dagger had pierced her heart and that her breath was being sucked out of her body. She quickly sat up and as quickly, fell in agony to the ground, sobbing.

When she was fully awake, Shaahatuck realized she was shouting. She was frightened and ashamed. If the enemies were in the area, they would have found her, and then the rest of her tribe. She crawled into her cave, curled into a fetal position, cradled her belly and tried to calm herself. As sad as it was, she believed in spiritual dream interpretation, so she analyzed her dream:

The snow represented the clouds, so Manassaquoit must be dead. Her heart almost stopped beating at the thought, but she continued her analysis: The snow in her hands represented her future children. The snow turned to ashes, because any future children would go to the fire with Manassaquoit, if he were indeed, dead.

Shaahatuck caressed her belly, comforted by the feel of her slightly swollen body. She said to the tiny spirit growing within her, "At least I will have you if I am left alone." She closed her eyes and tried to go back to sleep, but was immediately aware of someone standing on the sand looking at her. Her heart almost ceased to beat. She clutched her belly and tried to move farther back into her cave, but could not move. Finally, she realized that the person was a young woman about her own age. The woman spoke, "Shaahatuck."

Shaahatuck asked, "How do you know my name? Who are you?" Suddenly, she realized that it was the spirit of her mother, Powhantuwa. At first, she was frightened, for no spirits had ever visited her.

The spirit of Powhantuwa spoke. She said, "I will be with Manassaquoit." The spirit disappeared. Shaahatuck felt peaceful, feeling assured that Manassaquoit would return to her through the grace of her mother. She reasoned that her dream was probably just her own fears becoming vivid. Manassaquoit was a strong man. He was braver than anyone she knew. He would be fine. All would be good. The gentle falling of autumn leaves brought her out of her reverie.

Reminiscing about her life with Manassaquoit had been a wonderful distraction, even if it ended with a nightmare. She supposed the vision of her dead mother was also only in her dreams. Even though it might have been a dream, it was still reassuring. She convinced herself all was well and her beloved would be back in her arms very soon.

Recovering, she continued her prayers through the night and even into the dawn. Somehow, she felt better in the morning. The fear had past. Her spirit was actually elated. To her, it was a good sign. She felt everything would be all right. Reassuringly, she said aloud, "Today, they will return. I just know it. We will be together again. Soon we will remember the day we became one. We will celebrate. I can tell him what I am sure he already suspects. We will celebrate our little one."

It was the season of the fifth anniversary when Shaahatuck entered the wigwam of Manassaquoit. There was a full moon at night, and then a beautiful sunny morning. Looking down, she smiled and began caressing the sand with her bare feet. She remembered the autumn leaves, sand, and flowers on which they stood as the Chief proclaimed they were one. She sighed joyfully, "What a wonderful time. When the leaves fell soft upon my face, I was, forever, His." She hugged herself in gentle, sweet remembrance.

So sure all was well, Shaahatuck felt bad for leaving the compound and the protection of the tribe. She knew Manassaquoit and Chief Manakouk would be displeased with her. She decided to return to the temporary camp. While tying her sandals, she rehearsed her defense, "If anyone questions my absence, I will say I went away from the crowd to pray alone and lost my way." Then she reprimand herself, "No, they would not believe me. I will not lie to Manassaquoit. I will say nothing. If anyone questions me, I will just stare at them." She hurried her preparations to leave the beach and return to the sanctuary of the forest. She was no longer worried. Her soul was at peace.

CHAPTER THREE
From Nightmare-Awake

Earlier, far up river, the exhausted joint chiefs held their right hands high. A young man held a feathered staff high for all the warriors to see. A young guard cupped his mouth and signaled, **"Victory, Halt the Battle!"** The wounded and dead bodies of their comrades, along with the dead Shanaquoix, were covering the fields. The fowl of the air were gathering. The battle was over.

The tribes gave thanks to the Father Spirit for helping them protect their land and their people. They prayed for the souls of their dead, and the dead of the Shanaquoix. They doctored their own wounded. Each chief gave orders for his own braves to secure their dead and wounded on horses. They, jointly left a large band of braves from each tribe to guard the northern shore, and then parted company.

Manassaquoit and Tucahaunna joined their father at the front of the line. Chief Manakouk was proud of his sons. They were heroic, leading the battle straight into the enemy lines, and fighting alongside the other warriors. They had, if only temporarily, protected their homeland, but were exhausted from battle and had depression for their dead.

Manassaquoit rode silently. He wanted to return home to Shaahatuck. The thought of lying next to her, making love to her was a passionate incentive to hurry home. Her face was all he saw as he rode. He wondered if there was a little one in her belly. He was sure there was. This thought he wanted to share with no one. Being deep in thought, he did not notice the rustling of bushes along the trail. Suddenly, a young Shanaquoix defector jumped out of the bushes and shot an arrow directly into his chest. Manassaquoit clutched his chest and tumbled from his horse, falling on the arrow, driving it deeper into his body.

Chief Manakouk held up his right arm as a silent command, "Halt!" Tucahaunna instantly jabbed his heels into the side of his steed and went after the attacker. He stopped directly in front of the young man and stabbed him in his heart. Manakouk immediately jumped from his horse and went to Manassaquoit. He cradled him in his arms as if he were a child. Manassaquoit looked at his father. When he saw the spirit of Powhantuwa also kneeling by his side, he realized he was mortally wounded. He tried to plead, "Take care of Shaaha…" With those unfinished words, he took his last breath. Powhantuwa took the hand of her son-in-law and led his soul to the Father Spirit.

Manakouk continued to hold the head of his son on his lap. He wanted to wail, to scream words of torment and curse the young attacker, but he remained silent in his grief. Suddenly, he remembered a vision of Hatsawa while she was still pregnant with Manassaquoit. In her vision, she saw Manassaquoit being killed in the same manner.

The assembly began their journey home. Brothers and friends led the horses, carrying their dead and wounded, home. The horse of Manassaquoit, bearing his master's body, and led by Wapaughna (Waa-paw-na), marched directly behind the front line. The rest of the assembly flanked the horses carrying the dead and injured, to protect them from hungry animals.

The chief was proud of his warriors. They had fought a good fight. He called them 'Mighty Choptank.' He knew that when the tribe chanted and prayed for the souls of their dead, he would chant the loudest. He was proud to be their chief. He rode in silence, with his body facing forward and his face stern. He dared not to look back to the horse carrying his beloved first-born son! His brave son! The memory of his mate Hatsawa, and her vision, haunted him as he rode. Yes, Manassaquoit was a slain leader, but at that moment, he was, indeed, the beloved son of Chief Manakouk.

CHAPTER FOUR
Alone

J ust as Shaahatuck was preparing to leave the river, she heard the sound of galloping horses. She crawled back into her hideaway. She worried that, if the Shanaquoix had conquered her tribesmen, they would be coming to slaughter the remaining members of her tribe. She dared not look out to view the passing parade. Only when the sounds of the galloping horses were fading away, and all the riders were looking forward, did she dare to venture out to take a quick look. She recognized the men. They were her people. In her excitement, she forgot about going back to the forest.

She ran toward the procession, yelling, "Manassaquoit! Manassaquoit!" Her heart was glad again. She felt a surge of joy as she ran to the head of the line. Her yelling startled the line of already weary men. They turned to see her running past them. Shaahatuck saw no sadness, no bodies on horses. Her eyes were fixed on the front line.

Chief Manakouk held up his hand. The procession came to a halt. He demanded, "Daughter, why are you here? No sound has been made to call you out of the forest." Shaahatuck could always smile and tease the old chief. He loved her. She was special to him. However, he said no more. He could not. To avoid witnessing her pain, he turned his face away. Stopping abruptly, Shaahatuck painfully looked up at her father-in-law. She saw only one son.

Struggling with the words, she feebly inquired, "Where is Manassaquoit? Where is Manassaquoit?" Her voice began getting louder, more desperate. She again begged, "Father, where...is..." As she stepped backward, she stumbled into the formation and against the horse of Manassaquoit. On its back was the expired body of her beloved. Her head exploded in pain. Her body gave way to extreme shock. She fell faint, to the ground. For her, the rest of the day was hazy.

The tribal members returned from the temporary camp and

gathered on the riverbank. They placed the bodies of the deceased on burial beds established along the shoreline, and waited for Manakouk's command to light the funeral fires. Chief Manakouk allowed Shaahatuck to be alone with Manassaquoit's body while the funeral fire beds were being constructed. When it was time for the funeral, Tucahaunna had to hold her, so the young men could take the body to the bed of straw.

Members of the tribe were sitting with loved ones, chanting prayers, crying, holding their babies and again chanting. Nothing would take away their grief. Nothing could take away the grief of Shaahatuck. She had no parents or siblings to comfort her. Chief Manakouk, and his remaining son, Tucahaunna, was only her adopted family.

Tucahaunna would someday be chief. He had not yet taken a mate. Thoughts of the future chief initiated an instant rush in Shaahatuck. She began wondering if Chief Manakouk would expect her to be the mate of Tucahaunna. However, she knew the heart of Tucahaunna belonged to another girl who would become his mate as soon as she became a woman. Besides, everyone knew, or thought they knew, the shame of Shaahatuck and her barren state. No man would want her. It did not matter, for she wanted no other man. She was not ready to share the secret that she was not barren.

With tears and dust falling into her mouth, Shaahatuck looked to the tall beds of sticks and straw, and tried to chant. She could not take her eyes from the lifeless body of Manassaquoit awaiting its purification. She knew that in a few minutes, he would begin his journey across the river into the clouds. She meekly whispered, "Do not go. Do not leave me Manassaquoit. Please do not leave me. You promised you would return. You said we would go to the Father Spirit as old ones together. Please let this be a dark dream. I want to open my eyes and see you. Then, I will go back to sleep in your arms."

Realizing the impossibility of her dreaming, Shaahatuck wanted to bury her face in the sand. She resisted. She did not want to lose one precious minute in view of her love. Her mind was racing with images of their life together. She wondered if all remembrance of their love would also go into the fire. She could not bear the thoughts of not having any memory of him. She just wanted to run away.

With a sadness in his eyes, Chief Manakouk looked to the family members who had lost loved ones. He looked at Shaahatuck, and then sadly lit the first fire, the one of his treasured son. Shaahatuck covered her mouth with both hands, to keep from screaming. Following Manakouk, other members began lighting the beds of their deceased loved ones. Soon the riverbank was full of fire and flames. The chanting became louder and louder. They were praying for the purification of their dead family members and for their journey to their final resting place with the Father Spirit. Still, their hearts were full of anguish.

Shaahatuck tried to find peace in the purification process for the sake of Manassaquoit. She may have been in mortal grief, but she believed in the teachings of her people, that, at the end of their earthly journey, they would go to live with the Father Spirit. For that day, the only thing she could deal with was the loss of Manassaquoit.

The entire tribe stayed by the burning bodies until the fire consumed the flesh from the bones and the tall stilts collapsed. They put out the flames. While the ashes were cooling, the tribe sent many prayers to the Father Spirit. Each family sifted through the ashes of their love one. They gathered the bones, and buried them, along with the ashes, on the higher grounds of the riverbank, in view of their blessed river.

Chief Manakouk chose a spot high on the bank as the resting place for the bones of his son. He and Tucahaunna gathered the bones of Manassaquoit. Shaahatuck could not bear to do so. She wanted to be alone. She walked away, and went to the burial site of her mother, Powhantuwa. She gathered two large shells that her mother had brought back from the Great Waters, and that Shaahatuck had laid on the grave years ago. She took the beads of Roanoke and Wampum-

Peak from her neck and gently laid them in one of the two shells. She covered it with the other large shell. She wrapped the shells with layers of animal skins she had carried with her, alternating them with very thick mud. She added dried leaves, and then, more mud. Manakouk and Tucahaunna watched impatiently, as Shaahatuck added more skins, and finally another wet leaf/mudpack. She gave no explanations, but simply laid the package on a flat rock, in the warm sun. They thought she planned to put the shells in the grave. They were confused, but remained patient.

Shaahatuck finally explained, that she planned to let the mud-packed shells harden in the sun, and then, to bury the cocoon alongside the grave of Manassaquoit. The two men continued with the burial, filling the grave with many small stones. They gathered sand, poured it on the stones, and then added more stones. After the grave was totally filled and covered, they walked away to give Shaahatuck a few minutes alone. She methodically scooped up a handful of sand, and let it sift through her fingers. Feeling as if her life was slipping away with each grain, she began smoothing the sand, wetting it with her falling tears. She chanted mournfully.

The gritty sand was a stark reminder of the reality of the day. As if hoping everything was a bad dream from which she would awaken, Shaahatuck made one last plea. She cried, "Manassaquoit, please find some way to send your spirit back to me. I cannot live without you. Please, Manassaquoit, please don't leave me." She fell against the hard bed of stones, and sobbed until she was sick.

Finally, she gathered her 'package' and went to her wigwam. Keeping the shells close to her, she fell asleep. The next morning, she set it out in the sun to dry. She repeated this for several days and nights, sharing her grief with no one. When the package hardened a few weeks later, creating a cocoon, she secretly buried it in the grave of her beloved.

CHAPTER FIVE
A Mate for Wapaughna

few weeks after the death of Manassaquoit, Chief Manakouk called Shaahatuck to his wigwam. He began, "Shaahatuck, you have no parents or a mate. I have been your father, but I grow old. My Hatsawa is gone. I know it has been a short time since Manassaquoit has gone to be with the Father Spirit, but…"

Shaahatuck suspected what the chief was going to discuss with her, just not with whom. She wanted to scream aloud, but she cried inwardly, "Stop."

Chief Manakouk went on, "I need to provide for you. You need a man to take care of you. I would like to give you my son, Tucahaunna, but I know he has love for another girl who will be his mate. It is a great love, like the one you had for my first son." The words were sticking in the grieving chief's throat. Sadness began to threaten his logic, but he continued, "Like the one Hatsawa and I had for many moons. I want Wapaughna to take you for his mate. He is a brave man and a good hunter. He already has three children. You love them as their teacher, now you can be their mother.

Manakouk, trying to comfort his daughter-in-law, said, "Wapaughna will provide well for you. He loves you as he loved Manassaquoit. He will honor the memory of his friend by taking very good care of you. I have told him to be kind and patient with you. He said he would try very hard to make you happy. It is the time of the full moon. When Tucahaunna takes a mate, you will also become the mate of Wapaughna."

Shaahatuck wanted to yell out to her father-in-law, "The full moon? No!" She kept silent. She knew he had made the difficult decision for her welfare. That was it, sleeping with her mate's best friend. She cried in her soul, "This is too soon! Too soon! That full moon was supposed to belong to Manassaquoit and me. She inwardly lamented, "Not now, please not now."

As if reading her mind, Chief Manakouk sadly continued,

"Wamquwa is very much alone since he lost his mate last season. He has not looked at another woman. His heart is still sad. Her sickness took her quickly. I have watched you with the children. They already love you. The young girl will learn from you. You will nourish the sons with your cooking abilities, so they will grow into healthy braves. You will be good for them. They will grow to love you as a mother and you will be fulfilled as a parent. In time, you will grow to love Wapaughna."

Just like that! She would be good for them. It was not about her after all. It was for the good of Wamquwa's family. She silently questioned, "I will grow to love?" She added, "How do I grow to love. I already love. I was born loving Manassaquoit. My love just grew stronger. I could never love another." She was silently crying; her mind was racing. She inwardly cried, "What will I do? What will I do? Not this full moon. Oh please, not this full moon. This moon belongs to Manassaquoit and me. Let me at least have that. Oh please, Father Spirit, let me have that."

Shaahatuck saw tears swelling in the eyes of her father. In her entire life, she had never seen him display such a sad emotion in the presence of any tribal member. He was always in charge of everything, including his emotions. If he ever shed a tear, he must have done so in the privacy of his own wigwam. She felt so ashamed. She knew he was grieving Manassaquoit as badly as she was. However, he loved her as a daughter, and was responsible for her welfare. She knelt down in front of the man who had been the perfect father, even before her birth father died. She said, "Father, I know you love me. I know you do what is best for me. I will obey you. I will become the mate of Wapaughna if that is what you wish. I will nurture his children; they will become mine" Chief Manakouk gently touched her cheek, and then called out to summon Wapaughna to enter the wigwam.

When Wapaughna entered, he smiled at Shaahatuck. She was still kneeling in front of the chief. He held his hand out to her. His smile seemed to be saying, "I am sorry for your loss. I will take good care of you." Shaahatuck took his outstretched hand, stood up and then dropped her hands by her sides.

Chief Manakouk said a few words to the couple, and then put Shaahatuck's right hand in the right hand of Wapaughna. Wapaughna put a string of Roanoke around her neck. They were engaged.

Manakouk dismissed Shaahatuck from the two men's presence. She was no longer needed. The men would work out the details of her future. She stumbled out of the wigwam as if in a trance, sadly thinking that Wapaughna would become the father of Manassaquoit's child. She kept repeating, "How can this be? How can this be?" Her stumbling became a quick pace, and then, a run. She began to sob very loudly. Needing to escape her emotional pain, she began running as fast as she could through the trees.

The events of the past few days and the thought of sleeping with another man so soon after losing Manassaquoit was too overwhelming. The next day was her wedding day. Her heart was breaking, for she could not share her secret with anyone. She truly wanted to please Chief Manakouk. He felt he was making a good choice for her life. As she ran, she sobbed as she remembered the events that drove her into the forest, and to the anguish of the day.

She painfully went into labor and lost the precious baby she and Manassaquoit had long been awaiting. She wailed as she delivered the little one onto the cold musty ground.

Even in her anguish, Shaahatuck recognized the importance of purifying the remains of her baby. After she did so, she feared animals would soon get a scent of new birth. She hurriedly went to the river.

Memories aside, she needed to attend to her baby's journey to the Father Spirit.

Reaching an isolated portion of the river, Shaahatuck held the tiny bundle, containing the ashes of her newborn baby, over her head to keep it dry. She walked into the river.

Alternating the bundle from hand to hand, she washed the evidence of birth from her body and clothing. Although baptism was not a common practice, she cupped her hand, gathered a small amount of water from her precious river and touched it to the tiny package. She prayed for blessings for her 'son' and then walked out of the river and up to the fresh grave of Manassaquoit.

Struggling with the piles of stones, she excavated the top portion of the grave and retrieved the large cocoon, which she had secretly buried only a few weeks before. The sight of other stone sickened her. She knew the bones of Manassaquoit were just below them. Furtively, she began to claw at the stones, taking them out of the grave, one by one. Hysterical, by this time, she stopped and wrung her sore hands until blood began to ooze from them. She dropped her head and held her face in her bloody hands, finally falling onto the grave and sobbing wildly.

After allowing her anger and depression to be released through her sobbing, Shaahatuck was able to regain composure long enough to realize what she was doing was an abomination to the Father Spirit. She was unnecessarily disturbing the sacred burial site of the most important person in her life. She wiped her tears and picked up one of the larger rocks. Using it as a tool, she quickly opened the original shell, caressed the tiny package containing what she hoped were the remains of her baby, and then deposited it in with her betrothal and marriage necklaces. She wept as she carefully re-wrapped the shells with layers and layers of mud, leaves and sand. She returned the rocks. Finally, she covered the grave with dirt and more stones.

Enduring the emotional anguish of re-opening the grave, she buried the cocoon for the last time. Exhausted from emotional and physical pain, she went back into the river, bathed and went to her wigwam and tried to sleep.

CHAPTER SIX
Wedding Day

Memories of the previous month were vivid in the mind of Shaahatuck. In her wretched state, it seemed so long ago. So much had happened. She had experienced so much anguish. She spent the night in remembrances, which haunted her to the point of tears.

She remembered, with severe hatred, the vision (or dream) of her mother, Powhantuwa, that she experienced while Manassaquoit was at battle. On that day, she was encouraged that he would return to her through her mother's loving spirit. She had never experienced a vision of her mother. Therefore, she took that as a good sign. She misunderstood. The spirit of Powhantuwa was merely a messenger to escort Manassaquoit to the Father Spirit. Her message to Shaahatuck was that he would not be alone. Shaahatuck had always been taught to pray for the spirits of the deceased loved ones. That night, she could not pray.

Even though Powhantuwa, while still alive, had a short period of unsatisfactory mothering after the death of her mate, she recovered to be the perfect mother to the young Shaahatuck. Powhantuwa was her source of love and gentleness. However, the love for Manassaquoit was stronger than any other love. She still felt angry and betrayed. Sleep would not bless her because she knew that thoughts of hatred for her mother's spirit was another abomination to the Father Spirit. She tried to pray; prayers would not come to her. She tried to sleep; sleep would not come to her. The only thoughts that haunted her were those of her life with Manassaquoit. She repeated words he spoke to her, felt his arms around her; smiled at the remembrance of his smile and so much more.

She felt sad for Manakouk. The knowledge that she had aborted his grandson disturbed her. She had already decided not to tell him about it, as it would only add to his grief. Morning came too soon. She awoke before the morning light.

It was a beautiful, warm, peaceful morning. The leaves were beginning to turn a golden brown. The aroma of a meal being prepared, usually a wonderful welcome to morning, saddened Chief Manakouk. He sat alone by the morning fire. As if trying to distract his own mind from its grief, he turned his thoughts to duty. He forced himself to say, "Time for the harvest. We will reap the corn after the joining feast. Soon the entire tribe will arrive, and the ritual will begin. We will be blessed."

Many young girls had come of age. They and their braves wanted to be together before the snows came. Manakouk held his head in his hands as he thought about the fact he would also be giving away his only daughter, the mate of his beloved Manassaquoit.

Suffering the pain of losing his son caused Manakouk to remember his mate, Hatsawa. His mind wandered, again, to her vision of an arrow piercing the heart of Manassaquoit as he rode on a horse. He remembered his words to her, "Just a bad dream." She truly saw into the future and witnessed her own son's murder. It grieved him that she did not live to see what handsome and vital braves her sons became. The thought of her vision, of the murder of her first-born son, snaked throughout her life, even to her deathbed.

As Manakouk remembered their life together, he smiled and thought, "Oh, how we loved. She was my best friend." They were of the same tribe and knew each other their entire lifetime. Hatsawa always wished to be his mate. Manakouk took it for granted she would be, and did not even ask her to join with him until his father urged him to do so.

The crackle of fire and the activities of the morning brought Manakouk out of his reverie. He forced himself to say, "What will be, will be." He hoped that in spite of Shaahatuck's grief, she would meditate on her unity with Wapaughna. He felt compassion for her, regarding the decision he had made, but he could not regret it. It was for her good. Still, he felt sad for her.

It was a beautiful day after the previous night's full moon,

Wapaughna and Shaahatuck's Wedding Day. Shaahatuck walked out of her wigwam and looked up to the sky. After saying her morning prayers, she looked over to the far side of the camp. Wapaughna was gathering fresh leaves, and laying them out to dry in the sun. She knew he would place them on the ground inside his wigwam, and cover them with beautiful soft skins to provide a marriage bed. His problem was solved. He would have a sleep partner and a mother for his children. To her, it was still a time of mourning, the day after the birth, death and burial of Manassaquoit's son.

As she looked at the wigwam in which she would spend her wedding night, Shaahatuck cried, "It should not be. It should not be." The thought of Wapaughna touching her already pain-ridden body was too much for her to bear. She planned to go through the motions of preparing for the ritual to unite them, but it would only be that, just motions. She was extremely sad. However, she decided she would make the effort for the sake of Manakouk.

She vowed that she would bathe, gather her belongings and throw away her bed covers. That night she would enter the wigwam of Wapaughna. She really wanted to please her revered father and chief. She secretly hoped Wapaughna would consider her grief and respect her mourning period for a while, but seriously doubted it. He had been without female companionship for a year. He was ready for a sleep-mate. She sadly walked to the river.

Yvonne Dorsey

CHAPTER SEVEN
The Blessed River

The water seemed to be flowing more violently than usual. The rocks seemed to be crying out in response to the peal of Mother Nature, as the constant pounding of the water beat and beat against them. To Shaahatuck, they were crying for her. Canoes lay alongside the fallen trees, canoes Manassaquoit helped carve and create. She thought of braves that would probably enter them later, to go fishing for the evening meal. For them, life would go on. She walked slowly along the riverbank. She saw the cave she had dug and covered. It was still intact. Nothing in nature had changed. Time seemed to be standing still. She stood frozen for a moment, observing the sight of it all. She looked overhead at the beautiful autumn sky.

Fish were jumping. Birds were flying overhead. The sand felt warm. The feel of splashing water against her bare feet was soothing, but it reminded her of sexual moments with Manassaquoit, when they would walk the sandy paths, and then give in to their love. They would hide away from others in a secluded spot along the banks and make love. She always felt wonderfully wicked. She despondently smiled at that thought.

Everything reminded her of Manassaquoit. It had only been a short time since they stood on the same sand and clung to each other, yet those days seemed as an entire lifetime away. Her whole life had changed. She looked over at the place where she stood as the Chief pronounced, "Manassaquoit and Shaahatuck are one."

Shaahatuck silently cried, "How can I stand there and become another man's mate? How can I stand so near Manassaquoit and my baby and make promises I may not be able to keep? How can I? How can I?"

She continued to walk along the riverbank, away from everyone. She questioned the sky, "How could this be? How could this be?" She ran from the beach to the burial site. There, she fell and sobbed until she was sick. She just wanted to stay there with the remains of her family. Suddenly, she arose, and ran to the Prayer Rock. Sobbing, she laid her face on the cold stone.

After she had spent her tears on the giant pillar of stone, she rubbed the moisture all over the marks she and Manassaquoit created. She rubbed and rubbed so hard her hands were bleeding, yet her only pain was in her heart. She wanted to bury her pain deep into the cold boulder. Finally, she arose, and slowly walked back toward the beach.

When she felt she had run far enough, and was alone at an isolated portion of the river, Shaahatuck stood at the water's edge and very loudly cried to the sky, "Manassaquoit, Manassaquoit." She turned and stared back toward the graves of her beloved mate and precious little one, and sobbed again. Her only consolation was the image in her mind of Manassaquoit seeing his own son with the Father Spirit. She wanted to be with them.

The mist of the splashing waters caressed her face. She looked up to the high nest of piled up straw, home to the osprey. She longed to see her mother once again, and regretted blaming her spirit for the death of Manassaquoit. She softly cried to the spirit of Powhantuwa, "If only you would appear."

Feeling the warm autumn sun shining down on her face, Shaahatuck lovingly remembered the story told by Chief Manakouk, how he purposely named an osprey 'Manassaquoit', so he could be looking at it when his son came into the world, and could legitimately give his son a majestic name. She smiled at the remembrance.

Thoughts of Manassaquoit never again seeing the huge fish-eagles returning to their nests saddened her. She remembered Powhantuwa telling the story of Wamquwa, how he chose her name, Shaahatuck. A tiny bird had fallen (or was pushed) from a nest and landed on his lap. It died at the very moment of Shaahatuck's birth. He believed the gentle spirit of the bird entered the soul of his baby. At that moment, he was sure his child was a little girl.

Shaahatuck cried as she remembered her parents. Her life seemed so useless. Memories of her wonderful life on her beloved river were moving in and out of her mind. A velvety vision of a smiling Manassaquoit overwhelmed her. She felt his strong arms around her. It sickened her.

Tears swelled, rose up from her being, spilled over her cheeks, and fell, as raindrops, onto the earth. Feeling nauseous, she fell, and wiped her face with the warm, gritty, wet sand. She softly cried, "Manassaquoit, Manassaquoit. This should have been a beautiful day, our day. The full moon should have been our moon, our light of love."

She began to chant, but the chanting was not for her unity with Wapaughna. It was for her soul, the soul of Manassaquoit, and the soul of their child. It was for their love. She took off the beads of Roanoke that Wapaughna put around her neck, and let them fall. She arose and walked to the river's edge. She raised her arms in reverence, and begged the Father Spirit to take mercy on her, and allow her to join her only true love.

With the face of Manassaquoit before her, and being very devoid of logic, she stepped into the Mighty Choptank River which had nurtured their love. She cried out one last time, "Manassaquoit! Manassaquoit!" She kept walking until the river grasses became her newfound bed. The river accepted the body of Shaahatuck and continued to flow. **It would not be changed**. It would remain the Mighty Choptank. **A River of Love**!

A River of Tears.

Section Two

THIS MILLENNIUM

The Haunting of Shannon Fitzpatrick

Yvonne Dorsey

CHAPTER ONE
Haunting Vacations Memories

It was a Golden Leaf Tuesday in early October, the first week of the month-long vacation of Ian and Shannon Fitzpatrick.

Shannon was positive she saw a young girl running alongside the car. Her frantic, wild, dark, pleading eyes were staring through the passenger car window. She grasped the door handle. The feel of hard leather brought her to the reality of the day. She knew she was safe and sitting in the passenger seat of an automobile, enjoying a wonderful vacation on Maryland's Eastern Shore, but she nervously wondered about the vision. She was not sure of what really happened. Where she was during that frightful haunting moment? She held onto Ian's arm for assurance that she was still in his world. Ian pulled the car over to the shoulder of the road. He turned to Shannon and asked again, "Are you alright Luv?"

Shannon, trying to explain what she saw through the passenger window, said, "Ian I know I saw a girl running alongside the car, but staring at me at the same time. Her eyes were so dark and scary. She was closer to me than you."

Ian gently cupped her face in his two hands and said, "Shannon Fitzpatrick, no one is closer to you than me." Shannon's heart briefly quickened, yet softened. She felt suddenly sexual. She meekly smiled and nodded. However, the realization of the episode, or dream, caused her heart to pound. Her eyes, strained from the vision, were actually hurting. Her hand was sore from the tight grip on the door handle. She wanted to cry aloud. Instead, she laid her head on Ian's shoulder and tried to calm her shaking guts. Finally, she said, "I'm ok." Suddenly, she said, "Ian, do me a favor and back the car up a bit, will you please?" Even if she feared the outcome, she needed to probe the occurrence, hoping that possibly she had dozed off for a moment and had a bad dream. Ian did as she requested; he backed the car and parked it again. Nothing happened.

Ian got out of the car and retrieved two bottles of juice from a cooler sitting on the back seat. Shannon also exited the car. They sat on the grass alongside the road for about fifteen minutes.

Shannon really did not want to discuss the matter, but her outburst almost dictated that she tell Ian about her vision. Ian listened, but had no response. Shannon seemed to be calming. Thinking the episode to be over, he patted her knee and gently asked, "Are you ok to go on now, Luv?"

Shannon replied, "Sure." They got back in the car. As Ian began driving, she braced herself, closed her eyes tightly until she was certain they were beyond the area of the vision, but again experienced the strange feeling. She even imagined that she saw a shadow through her tightly closed eyes. For a while, Ian did not speak of it.

Before the alarming episode, the young couple were carefree happy go-lucky. Thinking the episode to be over, Ian joyfully proclaimed, "What a day! What a vacation! Good idea you had, Hon. When you suggested a month vacation, I thought you were off your rocker, but you were soooo right."

Shannon could not concentrate on casual chatter. The haunting incidence echoed in her mind. She remembered the sadness more than the fear. Even if Ian did believe she actually had an unexplainable encounter, he had no idea of the impact it had on her. To him, it was just a brief interruption in their tranquil morning drive.

Finally, deciding to discuss Shannon's experience, he began by saying, "These things happen sometimes. We may not understand them. They just happen. Maybe you're right, Shannon. Maybe you just had a quick bad dream. You'll be fine, Luv. We'll stop for the night. You'll be fine. You'll see." Shannon nodded, but in her heart, she knew something real and disturbing had just happened and she would not soon forget it.

Later that night, Ian returned to the motel room with a pizza. Shannon was curled up in a fetal position in the middle of the bed, sobbing. He could not understand her lamentations and was almost afraid to wake her. Finally, he gently touched her shoulder. Startled, she sat up, sobs still racking her body. Ian asked, "Honey, what's wrong?" By then he was concerned.

Shannon, slightly embarrassed by her actions, wiped her eyes and muttered, "I guess I just had another bad dream, Ian. It was the craziest dream. We were in a field, no, it was more like a beach and you were... Oh, never mind. It doesn't matter. Forgive my silly mood, Hon." Making an effort to tease and sound like her old self, she asked, "What in the world did we have for lunch? Whatever it was, it sure didn't agree with me, but that pizza sure will." She added, "What day is it anyway? Hey, you sure lose track of time when you're on vacation, don't you?" She nervously rambled on, while eating her pizza.

Ian smiled at the love of his life, deciding that her two episodes were merely results of a recent museum exhibit. Shannon was determined to put the episode behind her. She concentrated on their fun trip. The rest of their vacation was wonderful. They were like two kids at play. According to plans, their wonderful vacation completed their anniversary week. After a romantic and relaxing stay at a resort and spa, they enjoyed a fun filled drive back to their countryside home in western New Jersey. As they drove, they spent the hours reminiscing about their life together, especially laughing about the day they met:

Yvonne Dorsey

CHAPTER TWO
Shannon and Ian,
Their Beginning

The bright October sun glistened on the University Library steps.

Shannon Marie D'Arcy was lugging her heavy briefcase and laptop. As she struggled to take a sip of water from a bottle she was also juggling, she tottered on the steps, and dropped her briefcase. She also lost complete control of the water bottle, which was then, deposited on the wide marble steps. The same nasty water bottle splashed its contents on the head of a furious student.

Shaking his Irish auburn head, looking somewhat like a soaking-wet doggie, the student yelled in a thick brogue, "What the h...."

Shannon gathered her bag and bottle from the steps and mumbled the beginning of an apology. However, the sound of cursing and the sight of the auburn haired Irishman shaking his thick head of hair was just too funny. Grinning, she sat down on the steps and then looked up into the greenest, most compelling eyes she had ever seen. Her stomach tightened.

The Irishman just stared at her. His stomach churned. Trying to think of something clever to say and not succeeding, he asked, "Are you someone I should know?" Realizing how idiotic his question was, he tried to change it, "I'm sorry, you took me off guard with this shower. I did have one today, you know!"

Weak-kneed Shannon was having difficulty concentrating on the responsibility of an apology. Her entire body was vibrating and her heart was pounding. She actually felt scared. Quickly gathering her belongings, she did manage to mutter something of an apology, and then rode off on her bicycle.

As soon as she was alone in her bedroom, she fell on the bed and cried. She was not sure of what had just happened.

Something very significant did happen, and it was in the Irish person of

Ian Ryan Fitzpatrick.

Shannon was sure she would see him again, as he was attending the same school. Rewinding the events of their chance meeting, she began praying she would meet him again, yet afraid she would. Her emotions were going from smiling at the memory of him shaking his thick red hair, to a sick, fearful agony in the pit of her stomach.

Later the next day, at a small desk, in a study room at the rear of the library, Shannon sat, reading. A smiling Ian leaned across the desk. Shannon, who was trying to stay focused on her studies and failing miserably, looked up once again, into those green eyes and once again, succumbed to the new familiar, sick, scary feeling.

The Irish intruder said, "Excuse me, but I do think you are indeed someone I should know."

Startled, Shannon said, "Excuse me?" Then she added, "I don't know you."

An apologizing Ian said, "I know. I am sorry. Wrong approach I guess. Let me try again. My name is Ian Ryan Fitzpatrick. Will you marry me?" Shannon laughed aloud.

The librarian said, "Quiet."

That was their beginning: *A water bottle shower, marble steps, a desk, a marriage proposal, laughter and an exchange of smiles that melted each of their hearts.*

There was the bonus of a dormant passion in both of them, awaiting the right person to arrive with an activation kiss.

CHAPTER THREE
Family

The D'Arcy and the Fitzpatricks lived an ocean apart. Fate brought them together and created a strongly bonded family.

The D'Arcys:

Originally from Normandy, France, had lived in Ireland for centuries. Some of them moved to America. Many of them settled in West Virginia so the men could find employment as coal miners, the trade they knew in Europe. That was the case for the ancestors of Shannon Marie D'Arcy.

The earlier D'Arcys lived in Coal Camps in West Virginia. Coal Camp, a name given to a village of homes owned by the coal mining companies. Shannon's father, James, a coal miner, met, fell in love with, and married a redheaded West Virginia girl by the name of Kally Glenn. He wanted to move out of the area and work in a different trade, but Kally did not want to leave her homeland. James continued working in the mines. They had one child, **Shannon Marie**.

When Shannon was just seven years old, James, as his father before him, died in a mining accident. Kally was a young widow of twenty-five. She grieved, feeling her husband's death was a result of her reluctance to move away from the coal-mining region. She did not want her daughter to marry a coal miner, and knew she had to make an immediate decision for her future.

As much as it was going to sadden Kally, she knew she needed to leave her precious mountain state. She knew the coal mining industry was much safer than it had been in the past, and through technology, the mines were a safer workplace. Possibly, the truth was, she just needed a change. Therefore, she decided that they would move closer to the New York, New Jersey area. James's brother Brian and his wife Louise, plus a few friends, were already working in New Jersey.

She was surprised that, except for leaving her best friend, Holly, Shannon accepted the announcement as well as she did. Kally had the same emotion about leaving her best friend, Lori, (Holly's mom) but the decision was made. James's life insurance would ensure Shannon's future.

Six months later, regretfully, Kally and Shannon bade a tearful farewell to Holly and her parents. Lori cried as she watched her best friend, Kally, drive away. To her, and her family, it was as if their dear friends were simply moving out of their lives. Eight-year-old Holly, feeling that she would never see Holly again, spent the day in her room, her emotions changing from sadness to anger, then back to sadness again. It was too much for a nine year old to understand. Lori knew time would heal her daughter's wounds. Kally and Lori promised to keep in close touch and remain friends. They kept that promise. On that day, Shannon began a daily life journal.

When Shannon was seventeen, in her last year of high school, Kally became very ill, and died a short nine months later. Shannon's parents had made provisions to be buried in West Virginia. With the help of her Uncle Brian and Aunt Louise, Shannon took Kally home, to eternally rest next to James in the family burial plot. She and Kally, both victims of the 'Honey in the Rock' (coal) were returning to the gravesites of their fathers.

Standing at the graves of her parents, Shannon felt so alone. She was almost a young woman, yet felt like an orphaned child. She never thought of herself as being an orphan while Kally was alive. However, the day of the funeral, she did. It was a terrible burden for such a young woman. Kally's best friend Lori was inconsolable.

After Kally's funeral, Shannon, Holly and Holly's, boyfriend, Corey, stayed behind. They walked around the cemetery, touching the engraved names of family members on the stones. They sat under the giant oak tree, which gave shadow to James and Kally. Corey was actually Shannon's slightly older cousin. When they were children, and through correspondence, Shannon had often teased that, if Holly married Corey, she and Holly would be more than best friends; they would be relatives. Holly said she hated Corey, so that would never happen. Watching the couple holding hands during the funeral, Shannon did not think Holly hated Corey anymore.

Shannon and Holly promised to stay in touch. Brian and Louise invited Shannon to share their home while she finished school. She was able to graduate and save the money from Kally's life insurance. She worked for three years, until her savings equaled the cost of her education and living expenses. She would later declare, "God's intervention." The timing placed her in the right place at the right time, to meet the man who would later become her life.

The Fitzpatricks:

When Ian's father, Michael Fitzpatrick, was appointed Ireland's Ambassador to the United States, he and his wife, Kaitlin, were excited at the prospects of living in America, if only for a short time. Michael was an intelligent, but simple living man with a very responsible government position.

Kaitlin was sad at the thought of leaving her home, family and friends. However, she knew the time in America would afford their only child, Ian, the opportunity of extended studies abroad. Ian was in his senior year of Secondary School (high school), when his parents left for America. He stayed behind until he graduated, living with his father's cousin, Elisabeth and her family.

Michael and Kaitlin settled in Annapolis, Maryland. It was close enough to be near Michael's office in Washington, D.C., yet close to the bay. Their home in Annapolis resembled their home along the water in Ireland.

When the Fitzpatricks went back to Ireland for Ian's graduation, Ian accompanied them back to Annapolis. The plan was for him to attend studies in America, and then, when Michael retired, the three of them would return to Ireland.

After two years of basic studies in America, Ian enrolled in an advanced architectural course at a school in New York City. His life story changed. A chance meeting decided his destiny, and guided his future onto a new path. He met **Shannon Marie D'Arcy**. Ian Ryan Fitzpatrick and Shannon Marie D'Arcy were soul mates from the very beginning, from their first encounter on the steps of the library. They were rarely separated.

The D'Arcys and the Fitzpatricks Connect

One day, Ian, not being able to keep his joy to himself any longer, told his parents he had met the love of his life, his soul mate. He was positive it was God's plan for his life, pure serendipity. Upon hearing his news, Ian's mother smiled and asked, "Shannon, ye say? Is she from Ireland, Ian?"

Ian replied. "No, Mum, she's from West Virginia."

Kaitlin asked, "Where's West Virginia, Ian?" Without waiting for an answer, she continued, "You know, we will soon be returning to Ireland. Can't you wait to marry a proper Irish girl?"

Ian's only answer was, "No!" Kaitlin knew she could not change his mind. Michael did not even try.

Ian had already decided if Shannon would consent to marry him, but did not wish to move to Ireland, they would live their life together in America. Shannon was prepared to go anywhere with him. The deciding factor of where they would call home was the exciting fact that, immediately upon graduation, they both landed wonderful jobs in New York City. They settled near Shannon's relatives in New Jersey. Their apartment was on the ground floor, in the back of an old Victorian house owned by John and Bea Turner, who lived in the rest of the house. Ian began working with an architectural firm. Shannon became an assistant to a Theatrical Set Designer, Andrew Marshall.

In the beginning, Andrew was not too thrilled to be assisted by a woman, especially one straight out of college, but Shannon was the most qualified of all the applicants. For Shannon, landing such a responsible job immediately after graduation was both rewarding and scary. However, she felt she would be an asset to Andrew, and was confident she would win his respect. Eventually, she did. They became a very creative team. She could almost read his mind. He liked that...Sometimes!

Andrew and Shannon loved designing the many scenes needed for the productions. They usually worked late most nights for the entire week before the opening night of a new play. Working and eating, then working some more was the norm. Work would usually turn to giggles when they were both so tired they were silly. Seeing the fruits of their labor on opening night was their reward.

Ian and Andrew's wife, Jennifer, recognized the synergetic relationship between the two designers. The couples enjoyed dinner after each performance. Of course, there was always a volley of questions and answers, "Should we have done this or changed that, etc. etc.?"

Ian would usually ask Jennifer, "Will they ever be happy?"

Jennifer would usually laugh and reply, "Probably not. There are both such perfectionists!"

Kaitlin and Michael loved visiting New York and going to the theater. After learning that Shannon was an orphan, had worked to save money for college, and was a very determined woman, much like herself, Kaitlin grew to love her as a daughter. Michael loved her right away. They became a close family. The bonus was, at least, Shannon was of Irish descent.

The young couple's decision to wait a year to marry disappointed Kaitlin. They chose autumn for their wedding. They both loved the water; Shannon had grown close to Ian's parents. She suggested they get married outdoors, along the bay in Maryland. Ian's parents were thrilled. Ian and Shannon's families and friends were happy to travel from Maryland, New York, New Jersey and West Virginia to attend. They planned their vacations around the October wedding.

Shannon persuaded Ian that they should each write vows, and then later, enter them, and their wedding pictures, as one unforgettable document of their love, in an album. Years later, their children could read it, and know how much their parents loved each other. At first, Ian said it sounded wonderful. When he was trying to write his part of the wedding vows, he thought to himself, "OK it'll go like this, "Shannon, when you baptized me on the library steps, you showered me with love and hydroplaned right into my heart. I would not let you out." He asked himself, "That's going to be my vow? "NOT!" he decided. He reminded himself of the very deep, special and spiritual love he had for his future bride. Their vows had to be of a spiritual nature. He knew her words would be, so he convinced her, that they should write their promises together. He knew what he wanted to say, but the truth was he needed Shannon's creativity to say it. That was fine for Shannon, thinking he could save the levity for the wedding reception.

Under a golden autumn sky, Ian and Shannon stood on golden leaves along the shore of The Chesapeake Bay, as the pastor declared they were married.

Though Michael and Kaitlin lived in Maryland, and Ian and Shannon, in New Jersey, they spent as much time together as possible. Kaitlin and Michael kept hoping a grandchild would be joining the family. Ian and Shannon planned to wait five years. In the two years Andrew and Shannon worked together, they, and their spouses, became very good friends.

Just after the second anniversary of Shannon's employment, a phone call from Jennifer sent her into shock. Jennifer muttered, "Andrew is dead." Shannon could not believe what she had just heard. Jennifer was sobbing over the phone. Finally, she was able to tell Shannon that while they were on vacation, Andrew suffered a fatal heart attack. He was dead before the paramedics could reach him.

A promotion to the position of Lead Set Designer was the natural next step for Shannon, as she was second-in-command. She chose her friend, Kim, to be her assistant. She surely did not want to climb the ladder of success that way, but fate was fate. The two years that Shannon worked with Andrew had been a successful learning experience. She was eventually successful in her own right.

One night, on the second anniversary of her new position, Shannon and Ian were leaving the theater. A supportive Ian said, "Andrew would be proud of you, Shannon."

Shannon, pleased with her own accomplishments, said, "I can't believe I've been with the theater for four years." Then she added, "This also reminds me, my husband, we promised ourselves a month-long vacation for our fifth anniversary. Remember? Better start planning! Time is fleeting."

Ian teased as if he did not remember, "Oh yeah, the 'Plan.' We've only got one more year. Better hurry, huh?"

The plan they drafted early in their relationship included saving as much money as possible during the first five years of their marriage, design their dream home and have it built with cash, no mortgage. That dream was finally within reach. Unfortunately, Kaitlin was not destined to see the arrival of any grandchildren. She became ill, and died very quickly. Shannon mourned Kaitlin's passing as much as she did the death of her own mother.

With his beloved Kaitlin gone, returning to Ireland no longer seemed the right thing for Michael. He decided to work out a plan to stay in America. Ian was his only child, and Shannon had become more like a daughter. How could he leave?

Kaitlin's illness and death was devastating; the young couple had almost lost their zeal for their plan. Michael told them that Kaitlin would not want them to put their entire life on hold for long. He reminded them of her words, "Only grieve me for a little while."

When they reached the end of the fourth year of marriage, Ian and Shannon agreed it had been a wonderful journey. They would continue that journey of saving and planning for one more year. They were finally in the stage of property search and building...after their vacation.

That was the life of Ian and Shannon Fitzpatrick, up to the wonderful, but haunting month-long vacation.

CHAPTER FOUR
Haunting Revealed

S hannon and Ian returned from their vacation on Friday afternoon. Ian was refreshed and excited about their renewed commitment to their plan. He was very happy they had saved enough money to make their dream a reality, and anxious to look for property. Shannon was equally committed, and deeply in love with Ian, but she was not very refreshed. Actually, she was still disturbed about the vision of the young girl in an ancient First Native American garment, and the accompanying sad, feeling.

On Monday morning, Shannon resumed her routine of driving to the train station, riding the train, and then taking the subway to the theater district. She made her regular stop for coffee.

A familiar voice called out, "Hey, welcome home, stranger." It was Kim, Shannon's assistant. As Shannon walked into the shop, Kim put her coffee aside to give her a welcome hug. They paid for their coffee, and began their usual hike to the theater. As they walked, Kim asked, "Have a great time?"

Shannon answered with a very quick "Yeah, we did." Her short blunt answer took Kim by surprise. She knew Ian and Shannon had really been looking forward to their playtime alone. She also knew Shannon was secretly hoping that she and Ian would launch their family while they were on vacation, so she was convinced something was wrong. Shannon would not satisfy her curiosity. Rather, she gave highlights of her wonderful vacation as they walked to the theater.

The two young women had developed a very good working relationship, as well as a friendship. Small talk was very comfortable for them, so Shannon's reluctance to discuss her vacation was confusing to Kim. After work, at a near-by gym, the two friends exercised, and were swimming. Kim quizzed Shannon, "Ok, girlfriend, what's up?"

Shannon answered, "Not a thing."

Kim had said nothing about it at work, but she felt that Shannon needed, and wanted, to talk. Finally, she asked, "Shannon, is anything wrong?"

Shannon answered, "It's nothing really." They swam for a few more minutes, and then got out of the pool.

Deciding to assure Kim that she and Ian were ok, Shannon finally confessed, "There was one little incident that upset me."

After relating the story to Kim, Shannon said, "It seems ridiculous to even discuss it. It was all so silly, but I had a strange feeling I was being haunted. I really spooked Ian. We laughed about it later. Sometimes I think I'm just too theatrical. Maybe I should have been on stage instead of behind it." By the time they left the gym, and parted company, Kim was satisfied her friend, and her friend's marriage, was ok.

Sharing her experience with Kim had a soothing effect on Shannon. Even in the crowded train and the drive home, she was at peace. As she entered the driveway, the sight of Ian raking leaves made her smile. She especially enjoyed the days when Ian was home before her. It gave her a warm feeling of home. She often said to him, "You sure make a lot of friends on the train."

Ian's reply was always of a cautious nature, "Shannon, please be careful to whom you speak, ok?"

Shannon would teasingly ask, "To whom I speak?" On most occasions, she thought he acted like a downright, cursing, roguish Irishman, and other times a fitting professor. Either way, he was fine by her. He made her laugh.

CHAPTER FIVE
The Bookstore

It was late October, a wonderful autumn, the time of year that made Shannon to want to dance, to play, to walk in the fields, or to toss leaves at Ian as he tried to rake them. He would usually give up and tackle her to the ground. They were like two children at play. Indeed, autumn was Shannon's favorite time of the year. However, the smell of autumn leaves was also a bittersweet memory of her mom, Kally, who always said. "A peaceful calm before the storm."

Ian and Shannon were enjoying their successes, their home and especially, their weekends together.

One October Sunday, Ian sat properly in the armchair, reading his section of the newspaper. Shannon was curled up on the couch, reading another section. Ian said, "I can't believe it's been a year since we were in Ocean City."

Shannon looked up from her portion of the paper and asked, "What made you think of that?"

Ian answered, "This article I'm reading on blue crabs." He turned the paper around for her to see.

Shannon smiled and said, "A magical month. Wasn't it? We should plan to go back there again, before we start house building. We're off schedule, anyway. Who knows, maybe we'll come back with a baby to be."

Ian cautioned, "Whoa, Mrs. Fitzpatrick, we haven't even found the perfect property yet and…" His voice began trailing off, when he realized he had deeply hurt his lover. His voice softened, "I'm sorry Luv. Shannon, I really do want a baby with you. Tell you what, let's get really aggressive." He lunged at her.

Shannon teasingly asked, "About property or baby?" Ian laughed as Shannon pulled him down on the couch.

As Shannon was leaving for the train on Monday morning, she asked Ian, "Will you be able to go to Matthew's book signing on Friday night?"

Ian answered, "Yes." He added, "I'll be driving in from my

Connecticut meeting, but I should be on time. Shall we meet at Kim's apartment? Are you going to take us a change of clothes?"

Shannon smiled at the redundant question because Ian knew her normal routine always included taking care of their social wardrobes and other details. She answered. "Sure, Sure. We need to leave her apartment by 6:45. Please call me if you're running late and we'll meet you at the bookstore."

The book signing was for author, Matthew Dwyer, a young professor from college. He became a mentor for Ian. The two men became friends, acting as best man at each other's wedding. Matthew and Sherry's wedding was a wonderful affair on a cruise around Manhattan. The party lasted until 4:00 am. Their friendship, forever.

Matthew was a very good photojournalist, but had not really published anything very income producing. Miraculously, but sadly, he happened to be at the destruction of the World Trade Center's Twin Towers in New York City, on Sept 11, 2001, to take pictures for an article he was writing. He experienced the devastation of that day. One evening over dinner, he told them, "It was not only destruction of buildings, but of personal finances, lives, families and spirits." He was very disturbed by it all.

While visiting, Matthew finally got up the nerve to give Ian a copy of his pictorial manuscript, his account of the horrible event. He invited them to the signing and to the party afterward. They had promised to go support him.

Matthew's book was especially important to him. He felt compelled to write his account of the disaster, and wanted to share his pictures with anyone who needed healing. He wrote nonstop for weeks, and revisited the site as much as possible to take pictures. The pictures he took were so emotive you could not look at them without tears in your eyes. By mid-October the manuscript was complete, and in the hands of a publisher.

Ian was very impressed with the book, and looked forward to the evening. His approval meant so much to Matthew.

Per the plan, Shannon and Kim went to the bookstore. When they arrived, Shannon made an apology to Matthew for Ian's tardiness. After a few pleasantries, she joined some friends in conversation for a short time, and then wandered through the store.

When she was alone, she mumbled, "It is almost 8 o'clock. Ian, you should be walking in the door by now." Her concern turned to anger, then back to concern again. She thought, "This is not like Ian." She tried to appear calm, but fear was rising inside her. She silently demanded, "Damn it, Ian Fitzpatrick, walk through that door. Where are you?" She managed to hold back threatening tears. By then, she knew something was wrong. Walking around the bookstore, she recalled Ian's earlier phone call. She remembered asking him,

"Are you going to make it early enough for dinner or do you want to wait and eat later?"

Ian had replied, "Later." He quickly added, "Hey, I've got some good news."

Shannon asked, "What?"

Ian interrupted her, "Oops, meeting's starting. See ya later Luv, gotta go, love ya."

Shannon replied, "Love ya back. See you tonight."

Shannon had a full schedule herself, and had no time for personal gab. She remembered thinking that Ian's good news would have to wait. Standing alone in the bookstore, she regretted the casualness of their conversation. Something was definitely wrong. She knew Ian was a very responsible person, and would have called if he could. She longed to see him appear in the doorway. Just his appearance always gave Shannon a warm gut wrenching feeling. How she longed for that feeling. Any feeling would have sufficed if he would just show up. She said aloud, "Darn you Ian Fitzpatrick!" At that moment, her insides were churning so badly she could not decide to be angry or worried, maybe both. She forced a smile across the room at Kim, who was obviously smitten with a certain young man, Keith, a young writer whom she met that evening.

Keith lived in New Jersey, but worked in SoHo, where the book signing was taking place. Shannon knew the excitement of the 'first encounter' and decided to keep her distance to give them privacy. "Privacy at a book signing? That's real private," thought Shannon. Knowing her friend and her friend's body language as well as she did, it was apparent that a relationship was developing.

Shannon decided to quit the door watching, and look for some good books. Half way down the aisle, she stopped. Something caught her eye. She gasped. It was a book with a beautiful young woman in ancient garb on the cover. She never read the book title. She saw another book about the Chesapeake Bay in Maryland. Suddenly, she recalled the vision of the girl running alongside the car. Her body chilled. She felt dizzy and uneasy. Panic re-visited her soul. Crying inwardly, she wondered, "Where is Ian? Did he have car trouble? No, he would've called."

She began wondering if her vision in Maryland was a premonition of Ian in danger. She called his cell phone the fourth time. The voice that usually gave her a wonderful jolt, spoke via a voicemail recording, "Hi, this is Ian Fitzpatrick.

Leave a message. I'll get back to you."

Shannon muttered, "You better get back to me, Ian Fitzpatrick." Her stomach tightened. She was scared. Then talking herself out of the feeling of Ian being in peril, she became angry. She knew how meetings could last and last. She mumbled, "But, he promised, damn it." She decided to buy the two books.

After paying for her purchases, Shannon visited with Matthew for a few more minutes. The evening was going well for him. He was busy. She was glad for the opportunity to leave. He signed her copy of his book. After saying her goodbyes, she secured a taxi ride to the train station.

As she prepared to board the train, her cell phone rang. Thinking, "Good, he's here," Choosing to be mad rather than fearful, she murmured, "Finally." She remained on the platform to answer the call. It was not Ian's number.

An unfamiliar female voice asked, "Mrs. Fitzpatrick?" The hair stood up on the back of Shannon's neck. Her heart was pounding.

She meekly replied, "Yes." The female voice stated, "This is Northwood Hospital. Your husband has been in an accident. Can you come immediately?"

The question angered Shannon. Of course, she would go right away, but she meekly replied, "Yes."

The very nice female on the other end of the phone line said, "When you get to the emergency room, ask for Michele, I'll take you to your husband."

Shannon felt ashamed for her angry thoughts against the person who had just called, but shame was not on her priority list. She could barely comprehend the conversation.

She hailed a taxi, and while en route to the hospital, made two phone calls: one to Kim, and one to her Uncle Brian. She decided to wait to call Michael until she had more details of Ian's condition. As she sat in the backseat of the taxi, she wrung her hands, and cried silently, "Oh God, Ian, don't leave me. Please stay with me. You promised we would build our dream house. We're supposed to grow old together, Ian. Remember? Please don't leave me!"

For that time, she only needed to know Ian was alive. She would later learn the details of his accident from the report by the surviving truck driver.

CHAPTER SIX
Heavy Steel

Ian Fitzpatrick was driving to the city to meet his wife, when a truck, carrying a load of steel pipes, unintentionally, forced his small sports car off the highway. The driver of the truck had suffered a massive heart attack and died at the wheel. The surviving truck driver was in serious condition, but recovered later, and explained the incident as it happened:

Due to the driver's heart attack, the truck was jackknifing out of control. The driving partner had managed to press the company's base-radio before he passed out. The truck rolled repeatedly, before coming to a stop in the ravine. When the base was unable to reach the truck-driving team by radio, they called 911.

Investigations proved that Ian tried to avoid a collision, by swerving to the side of the road. However, the truck followed the same path, barely missing his car. Pipes flew through the air. Only one or two steel pipes slightly touched Ian's tiny sports car, but it was enough to send it spiraling through the air. It landed in the same ravine. The accident destroyed his car, but more importantly, several bones were broken and he was in a coma.

For Shannon, learning that Ian was not speeding, but merely an innocent victim of an accident was reassuring. However, it did nothing to relieve her anxiety for Ian's survival. After signing the necessary papers and providing the insurance information for Ian's surgeries, she sat alone in the waiting room. She needed to cry, to wail, to sob, anything, but managed to keep her composure long enough to call Ian's father, Michael. Then, she listened, repeatedly, to a previous message Ian had made to her cell phone, just to hear his voice, exhausting the battery.

Kim arrived very quickly. Brian and Louise were there within an hour. Shannon sat in shock, wringing her hands.

Realizing she could be losing Ian, she regretted that they had decided to wait to have a baby. When sobs welling up inside her threatened to surface, she clasped both hands over her mouth to suppress them.

As comforting as it was to have family and friends with her, Shannon felt so alone. They sat, waiting for news of Ian's condition. Often, a nurse came and assured them Ian was stable. Shannon silently begged her father-in-law, "Michael, please hurry."

Michael's mind was racing as he prepared to go to New York. He barely remembered the flight. Looking out the window of the plane, he muttered, "Should've driven myself. Would've made better time." No mode of transportation would have sufficed.

Shannon's phone call barely made sense, "Michael…its Shannon…its Ian, He's hurt. Please come up." The only other information she could give him was the name of the hospital.

For Michael, there was no need for more information. Ian was hurt. Enough to know. Getting just the needed facts, he left as quickly as he could. The ride from the airport to the hospital seemed even longer than his flight. His heart was racing as the cab pulled up to the curb. He kept reminding himself, "Got to get my emotions in control for Shannon." By the time he arrived at the emergency ward, Ian was out of surgery, and in the intensive care unit.

At the sight of Michael coming into the room, Shannon began to sob. Trying to reassure her, as well as himself, he held her and said, "It'll be all right Luv." He let her cry on his shoulder, even before he approached his motionless son, lying only a few inches away. Brian, Louise and Kim left to give him and Shannon their privacy.

Later in the evening, Michael sat at the kitchen table in Ian and Shannon's apartment. Looking around the room, he smiled and reminisced about the day he and Kaitlin first visited the apartment. He felt it was too small and planned to offer financial assistance so they could afford a bigger place. Kaitlin gently reminded him about their plan. "Oh yes, The Plan," he would quietly tease his wife. However, he was extremely proud of the young couple.

The memory of Ian, with his head bandaged, and being in a body cast, haunted Michael. Memories of the days of dealing with Kaitlin's illness and death were rushing through his mind. He reminded himself, "At least Ian is alive."

October: Shannon purchased an anniversary card and a bouquet of flowers and put them on the table next to Ian's bed. Her constant companions, her Uncle Brian and Aunt Louise, Michael, Kim and Kim's new boyfriend, Keith, were often by her side. Her landlords, John and Bea, visited often with homemade goodies for everyone.

November: Thanksgiving month. Michael came for the weekend. He and Shannon ate their Thanksgiving dinner in the dining room of the hospital. They spent the rest of the weekend in Ian's room.

Several evenings each week, Kim stopped by to pick up Shannon's work, to give a progress report and to be of encouragement. Ian showed no signs of awakening from the coma. It was apparent he would still be in the hospital for the Christmas Holidays and maybe a lot longer, with no guarantee of his condition if, or when, he did awaken. Shannon began dreading the Christmas Holidays. Kim, always trying to sound encouraging, would often say, "He'll come around soon, Shannon."

December: Shannon saved all cell phone messages from Ian. She listened to them often. She wanted to hear his voice, but sobbed when she did.

Early in the month, Kim and Keith brought a table sized Christmas tree to Ian's hospital room. The decorations were sparse, so they added some of their own. They adorned the top with a beautiful Irish angel. Looking at the little cherub, Keith, trying to sound hopeful, said, "She'll make it all right."

Keith's gesture touched Shannon. She thought, "Poor guy, he never even knew Ian, now he's a constant visitor."

Shannon left the room for a few minutes. Kim, hoping Ian, even in his sleep state, could hear her, introduced the two men one night, "Ian, this is Keith. Keith, this is Ian."

Christmas: was Shannon's favorite holiday. She loved setting out a manger she hand painted. That year, there was no manger. Michael spent a week with her. He remembered how hard it was for him during his first Christmas Holiday without his Kaitlin. When she was alive, Ian and Shannon spent their Christmas and New Year's Holiday in Annapolis. Visiting there and Washington was always very exciting for the young couple.

The first Christmas after Kaitlin's death, Michael had visited New Jersey. He, Ian and Shannon did their best to have a beautiful Christmas without the presence of their dear Kaitlin. With Ian's comatose state, they saw no visible evidence of him awakening. It seemed they had also lost him. They reminded each other, "God forbid the thought."

Here they were; two people, who were total strangers a few short years prior, bonded by a common love and grief and spending the Christmas Holiday together. Traveling to and from the apartment and hospital was their holiday time together, but Michael was grateful for the time spent with Ian. He loved being in the apartment. Being around Ian's possessions gave him a small degree of comfort. He enjoyed the friendship of John and Bea, who only stayed a few minutes each evening to inquire of Ian's progress. They were both of Michael's generation and loved Ian and Shannon as if they were their own children.

While at the apartment, Michael usually sat at the kitchen table well into the night, praying for a Christmas miracle. One night, as he looked around the small room, he realized just how much Ian and Shannon enjoyed their country home. They maintained the yard for John and Bea. The elder couple were grateful for the maintenance.

Michael and Shannon had spent most of the Christmas

week in the hospital. Michael wanted to take Shannon out for dinner on Christmas Eve. Kim and Keith offered to sit with Ian, but Shannon could not bear to leave him for fear he would awaken and she would not be with him when he did. She had said, "Even worse, if he should…" Remembering the conversation, Shannon could not shake the remorse of hurting Michael. In her own grief, she had almost forgotten he also needed comforting.

New Year's Eve just came and went. Family and friends came by the hospital. On their way to celebrate their first New Year's Eve as a couple, Kim and Keith brought a small platter of food and a cappuccino. After they left the room, Kim said to Keith, "I hate leaving Shannon. It would have been wonderful if we were celebrating our first New Year's Eve with them." Keith, being supportive, reminded her of the doctors' prognosis of a temporary situation. Michael stayed through New Year Day. As he was leaving, Shannon felt bad for him, and wished she could have done something to make his visit better.

It was a new year, but the same circumstance. Doctor Loren released Ian to a short-term care facility for a period of three to five months, indicating there was a possibility of recovery. If Ian did not awaken by then, Shannon had to make other long-term plans.

Shannon spent her days going from home to the health care facility, and then to the theater. At day's end, she reversed the order. What a contrast! What confusion! The theater needed her full attention. She felt guilty. She was becoming distracted from her responsibilities. When she was there, she could not concentrate. Every other minute, she thought of Ian alone, wondering, "Is he choking? Is he all right?" She felt guilty leaving him for a full day. She was concerned with the facility being so far from their home, but reasoned that she spent most of her day in the area near the facility. Ian's body was healing, but he showed no signs of awakening.

Shannon felt the theater's cooperation was wearing thin.

She promised to be more hands on, and was trying hard to keep that promise, working at the theater four hours/four days, and then home one full day. She visited Ian for an hour each evening before going home, and spent her weekends sitting by his bed, working on her laptop. She was thankful the facility was closer to the theater than her apartment.

With the new plan, and Kim's help, she managed to finish the set designs for the season. However, her energy was waning and her faith severely tested. She knew the work arrangement was an imposition on everyone.

January, February and March: Ian slept. Shannon worked. Her friends and family visited as often as they could. Ian's stay in the short-term care facility was ending. The end of June was the cut-off date for insurance coverage in that capacity.

April: Kim and Keith announced their engagement. They planned their wedding for the next month.

CHAPTER SEVEN
Seasons of Change

Mid-May: Kim and Keith had a small, but elegant wedding. Shannon felt obligated to attend. Choking back tears during the entire ceremony, she knew she would not be able to stay to celebrate at the reception. The couple understood. As always, before retiring, Shannon recorded the day's events in her journal.

June: just happened. Suddenly, there it was. One excellent Saturday afternoon in mid-month. Shannon spent the morning by Ian's bed, working on sketches. She made entries in her journal and then left his room. She walked to the end of the hall to stretch her mind and body. As she looked out the window, watching couples interact, she thought of lost dreams. Struggling with the decision to take Ian home and care for him, she was scared. However, she reasoned that, with professional aid, she could do it and still keep working. She decided that she would apply for all the financial support to which she was entitled.

As she was about to give way to tears, Kim entered the hallway and walked up to her. Shannon simply turned to her and said, "Nine months seems like forever. It has been almost nine months since Ian's accident. He is getting great therapy. The doctors say there is no apparent brain damage. He looks as if is just sleeping. I'm running out of prayers, Kim. He just lies there. What am I going to do?" The determined courage she had at the beginning of Ian's new journey was declining. She asked Kim, "Do you think Ian will ever awaken?"

Kim answered, "Yes, I do." Then she asked, "Shannon, don't you think you should give up the idea of taking him home? They may be able to do more for him in a long-term care facility and maybe speed his recovery. He's getting excellent care now. You said so yourself. He would probably get even better care with qualified professionals. Don't you think so? You could work full-time and be able to afford the cost if the insurance doesn't cover everything...." Shannon's tired eyes just stared straight at Kim.

Kim knew she should not have started the conversation. She also knew she was digging herself into a hole with her friend and did not know how to get out.

Shannon finally spoke, "How dare you suggest that, Kim." She walked back into Ian's room, with Kim following. She added, "It would be like giving him away. I just can't think of that right now."

Kim pleaded, "Shannon, we are all worried about you. You need more time for yourself, if you're going to be any good for Ian."

Shannon nervously picked up the journal and angrily remarked, "How could you even think such a thing? I'll manage ok with him at home." She put down the journal, paced the room, and sadly looked at Ian. Kim was so sorry for upsetting her friend.

Shannon was sure she could manage, but at what expense? The thought that she might be alienating her friends, added to her fears. She knew she had to do something quickly. She wondered if Ian heard the conversation.

Ian could stay in the care facility as long as the insurance would pay. Then, Shannon would have to start withdrawing the monies they had worked so hard to save. The thought sickened her. Michael had offered monetary assistance, and though it would probably come to that, she hated the thought. A settlement from the trucking company would be a long way off, after Ian recovered or died. She needed a new plan, but her creative juices had stopped flowing. Ian would require most of her time and energy.

After much thought and prayers, Shannon knew she had to retire from the theater, and do free-lance work from home, to allow for flexibility in her schedule. She was sure she would find something to keep their income secure. She kept reminding herself of Doctor Loren's expectation; Ian would awaken. He felt confident in a recovery. Ian's brain waves were still active. Still, it was becoming more difficult to hold onto hope. The young Fitzpatrick's future seemed to be slipping away.

Making plans to take care of Ian at home required strategy. He was no longer a physically injured person, but a comatose patient, requiring care and therapy. After much paperwork and correspondence, Ian's insurance company guaranteed to pay for qualified, part-time, home care. They would pay a nurse to stay eight hours a day, five days a week. If Shannon wanted to care for him at home, he would have to have constant care. She agreed to the terms, knowing that, after a while, she would be on her own, evenings, overnight and weekends. She could hire another professional, but she would be financially responsible.

Finding out Ian's coverage under her family medical policy also provided, for a specific period, eight hours per day of care, was an answered prayer. Shannon applied for it, feeling confident in her decision. Sixteen hours a day, five days a week for a predetermined amount of time, was what she could get. She accepted it as a good thing. "I can do this," she thought when, on July 3, she signed the papers needed to take Ian home.

The months of July, August, September and October: were all spent with Shannon, her workspace, Ian, his equipment, and alternating nurses crowding the tiny apartment. The living room furniture was stored, and replaced with a bedroom for Ian. The nurses had access to the kitchen and bath. Shannon's living space was the small kitchen/dining area, and her bedroom.

For courtesy's sake, Ian's and Shannon's family and friends did not mention their anniversary in October. Every morning, Shannon assured herself, "Soon Ian will awaken and we will continue our dreams." That thought was supposed to keep her sane. However, after many months it ceased to be encouraging. She was getting angry more often and feeling dead inside. Even with nursing help, there was still so much to do. She wanted to work as much as possible when a nurse was there. She had the responsibility of taking care of Ian during the night. In the beginning, she rested in the bedroom while the nurses were on duty. Trying to work with someone else in the apartment during the day was next to impossible. Bea offered her office space in the main portion of the house. Shannon accepted, only going to the apartment to sleep until her care-giving shift began.

Even with the demanding schedule, Shannon was determined to create an income, to avoid depleting their savings. She did so with creative advertisements for businesses. She had an ongoing, but only a fair income.

After spending months with the new schedule and business, Shannon's sleep habits were severely impaired. Falling asleep in the armchair next to Ian's bed one night, she had a dream. In it, someone was drowning. Trying to grab the person, she felt their hand slipping from hers. She yelled to the person to hold on. Her own yelling awakened her. She sat up quickly and grabbed Ian. She was so sure her vision meant he was dying. She cried repeatedly, "Please Ian, hang on. Please hang on."

November was just another month. Michael came for Thanksgiving weekend. Family and friends stopped in for brief visits. Kim and Keith brought a welcomed dinner basket. They apologized for such a short visit, as they were going to Long Island to have dinner with Kim's folks. The tiny apartment was so crowded with Ian's necessary items and equipment, entertaining was very difficult, but Shannon was grateful for the constant affection of the young couple. Still, Ian slept.

Michael felt guilty taking Shannon's bedroom, but she insisted. She slept on the floor in a sleeping bag, next to Ian's bed. As usual, when it was time for Michael's departure, Shannon clung to him and he, as usual, tried to reassure her all would be well. She would pat him on his back and agree with him. They both hid their tears until they were out of sight of each other.

After only six months of care giving, Shannon was crying herself to sleep. Deep down, she knew she had to face the possibility that Ian might never awaken. She began wondering if Kim had been right about trusting his care to professionals. In the meantime, she knew she needed to take care of herself.

December and Christmas: Michael had been unable to spend Christmas with her, because of a trip to Ireland. Shannon had insisted that both nurses take some time off to spend Christmas Day at home with their families. She promised she would call one of them immediately if needed. She and Ian were alone on Christmas morning.

Even if Ian was in a comatose situation, she was thankful for the privacy they had. She could lie next to him if she chose, or cuddle him in her arms. She sat by his bed through the night on Christmas Eve. She opened the gift she bought him, and held it up as if showing it to him. It was an Irish Claddagh charm hanging on a gold chain. She spent the night clutching it in her hand, occasionally caressing it across his face or rubbing it against her wedding ring. She dozed and awoke throughout the night.

A few visitors came during Christmas Day, bearing small gifts, mostly food, but only stayed a few minutes. John and Bea brought her a Christmas platter from their dinner, and stayed only long enough to wish her a Happy Christmas. Although her landlords never complained, she wondered about the noise from Ian's machines. She often wondered if she should move. But where? She was feeling guilty because of the imposition on her family and friends. Sadly remembering her mom, she thought, "If only Kally were here."

New Year's Eve, mid-morning: Depression was clouding Shannon's mind. Ian had been in a coma for almost fifteen months. As she began taking down their meager Christmas decorations, she thought, "Now, another New Year coming." Wanting time alone to pack away the Christmas decorations, she gave both nurses New Year's Day and evening off, promising to call if needed.

After packing away the treasures, she sat on the floor watching their electronic picture album. When she came to the section of their wonderful month-long vacation, she stopped and stared at the smiles that seem to belong to strangers. No tears surfaced. She just sat and stared. She cried, "Oh Ian, another New Year's Eve without you holding me. I don't have my mom or Kaitlin and now, Michael is not with us." She continued to sit in the middle of the room, occasionally dropping her face to the floor. No sounds were coming from her, no tears shed. Nothing. She sat up and fixed her eyes on Ian. His electrical life support, the only sound she heard. She longed to hear his voice. Her tired eyes were heavy. She leaned her head against the armchair and quickly dozed.

A few minutes later, the sound of the doorbell awakened her. Cautiously checking the peephole, Shannon gasped. She could not open the door fast enough. A smiling Michael stood in her doorway. He teased, "Just thought I'd pop in for the New Year's Eve Morning. Is that all right, Luv?"

Hearing Michael's thick Irish brogue was like hearing the voice of her savior. Seeing him, standing in her doorway, with his arms outstretched was like being rescued from a burning building. She threw herself into his waiting arms and sobbed, "Is it all right? Is it all right?" Being comforted by her father-in-law's presence, she relaxed with her tea.

CHAPTER EIGHT
What Eastern Shore?

Shannon was thrilled with the Michael's unexpected New Year's Day visit. She decided to give him time alone with Ian and to take some for herself as well. After being sure Michael had necessary phone numbers, she left him in charge of Ian and went out for a drive.

As she drove, Shannon remembered Kim's words of caution regarding Ian's home care. She knew her friend was right. Caring for him at home was much harder than she thought. She knew she needed to make a special 'thank you' phone call to her. She thought, "What good friends I have. What would I do without them?" As she drove home, her mind was processing so many thoughts. The apartment was getting more crowded. She was getting used to it, but the sight of Michael and his luggage sharing her small space made her realize it even more. Even though she needed a bigger place, she simply did not have the desire to house hunt just for the sole purpose of space. She needed something exhilarating to keep her spirit strong, possibly a change. Realizing she was feeling so much better having her father-in-law with her, Shannon wished he lived closer to her. Suddenly, as if a bolt of lightning had struck her right in the head, she knew what she needed to do. She asked herself, "When am I the happiest?" Of course, the answer was when she was with Ian, but she was with Ian all the time and she was miserable. She reasoned, "I'm the happiest when I'm around water, actually the ocean."

She knew the Eastern Shore of Maryland would give her needed comfort. Being near water, she would feel alive again, have fond memories and be near the places where she and Ian had spent such a glorious month. She thought of Michael. He would have a pleasant drive to the shore rather than the air flights and could visit more often. On the way home, she practiced her selling job. After they finished their late New Year's Eve lunch. Michael settled down in the armchair with his coffee. Shannon started her pitch, "Michael, will you help me move to the Eastern Shore?"

A startled Michael asked, "What Eastern Shore?"

Shannon answered, "I mean, 'Your Eastern Shore,' the one in Maryland. I need to find peace if I'm going to be strong enough for Ian. I'm fading fast. I'm tired. I'm crowded. Working in New York City was our dream; it was Ian's and mine. I loved my job, but the city is now just a depressing place where I lost Ian." She started to cry.

Attempting to comfort his daughter-in-law, Michael said, "You haven't lost Ian, Luv. He'll be all right. You must believe in miracles." He still had such strong faith, even after losing his precious Kaitlin. Shannon remembered when she used to have that faith. She was no longer sure of it, but she knew she needed to hang on to something. She hated the thoughts of leaving her family and friends; still, she had peace about moving to Maryland. If Ian awakened, they could always move back. If he were taken from her, she would be in a place that had given her so much joy, a place where she still had him. She would be closer to Michael, whom she regarded as her own father.

Michael loved the idea of his 'kids' being closer to him. Two hours away was far better than four to five hours. He wished Shannon would consider moving to the Annapolis area. After all, there was plenty of water there, but it was Shannon's plan. He agreed to take her house hunting. Shannon explained that once she found a house, she would hire a live-in nurse from the local area. They concluded their visit with a new plan in play.

Kim was torn between believing Shannon was making a rational decision, and thinking she was taking on much more than she could handle. However, she offered to help while Shannon and Michael traveled to Maryland, suggesting that she and Keith take turns staying at the apartment at night, to allow the night nurse periods of sleep. Packing the apartment was the easiest decision. Most of the furnishing and décor items were already packed.

According to the plan, Michael picked up Shannon at the airport, and they were very quickly en route to Maryland's Eastern Shore. As they approached the Bay Bridge, Michael inquired, "Why the Eastern Shore?" Shannon never answered. She just looked at the familiar large blue sign to the left, 'William Preston Bridge.' As they crossed the bridge, Michael, oblivious to the fact that Shannon had purposely ignored his inquiry, pointed, "Over there's the Chester River. Just around the bend is Queenstown. I have friends there." Pointing to the right, he said, "Over there is the Eastern Bay." While his information was interesting, the truth was Shannon already knew all those facts. She was more preoccupied with the surge of thrill coming up through her being. It was an all too familiar feeling, one she had experienced for the first time when she was a very small girl:

Once, friends of Shannon's parents invited her family to join them for a week's vacation on the Eastern Shore of Maryland. The D'Arcys were still living in West Virginia, and Shannon had never seen an ocean. Since that first visit, the sight of one always left her breathless.

Remembering her parents, especially Kally, and thinking of Ian's condition, saddened Shannon and brought her out of her reverie. She realized Michael was continuing his lone conversation. She heard only some of his words. Finishing a thought, he asked, "So wouldn't you be better, closer to the city Luv?" Realizing he was getting 'The Look' he thought, "Why did I ask such a dumb question?" He asked, "Want to hand over some grapes to stuff in my mouth now, Shannon?" He smiled. She smiled, opened the snack bag and gave him some grapes. She knew it was not about grapes. It was his proud way of saying, "I'm sorry, and I'll keep my big mouth out of your affairs."

It was obvious to Michael; his daughter-in-law knew

exactly what she needed to do and where she was going. If he only knew, it was not really so clear to her. She just knew she absolutely loved the water, and was more serene when she was near it. Maybe she could handle things better if she had peace of mind; she needed to be near water, preferably the ocean. Probably, any water would have been pleasant, but she was familiar with Maryland's Eastern Shore.

As they continued their drive, Shannon began wondering if moving to the area was indeed the answer, or just a whim conjured up out of her sadness. She found herself wondering if she were actually using Ian's condition to make this move. She had loved her job, had many friends and enjoyed a good life. She certainly had been very happy living in New Jersey with Ian, and was near family, but there always seemed to be something compelling, almost beckoning, every time she crossed the Bay Bridge into the Eastern Shore. She was feeling confused, and her mind was going helter skelter as she thought, "Maybe this isn't the right thing to do. Maybe this is the biggest mistake of my life, of Ian's life! She added, "Oh whatever." She silently reprimanded herself. Her thoughts were causing her to become angry.

When she began doubting her judgement, Shannon knew she needed to retreat and relax. She announced, "Let's get a place to stay, somewhere between Cambridge and Ocean City. We'll be close to any area we want to check out."

Michael answered with a cheery, "Yes Mam." The big Washington Diplomat was just her majesty's chauffeur for those few days and loving every minute of it. They located lodgings at a charming inn.

As they entered the reception area, several eyes turned. Shannon thought, "Hmm, maybe they're Washingtonians, out for a little vacation. Maybe they recognize Michael."

Michael had a different perspective. He noticed an older couple and chuckled to himself. His first, Irish-devilish impulse was to keep them guessing. He mocked their probable scenario, "What was this old coot doing with this beautiful young chick?" However, he resisted the teasing impulse. He walked up to the reservation desk, and in his big Irish brogue, said to the desk clerk, "Young Man, we'll have two rooms please. My daughter-in-law, herself, wants one with a view. Just a room with a good bed will be fine enough for the likes of an old man such as m'self." That broke the silence. Michael's thick Irish brogue, made thicker for entertainment's sake, amused everyone in the lobby. Folks were chuckling. The old folks smiled.

Michael and Shannon began house hunting afresh early the next day. The drive to and from the Ocean City area was nice, but not productive. They looked at several houses. The ones that Shannon thought she might be able to afford, were not near any water. In addition, she realized Michael's drive to Ocean City would be very congested and just as tiring as the one to their home in New Jersey.

She anguished, "I thought I would find the perfect home for me and Ian and I would know it instantly. It might not even be here. Maybe it was a dream I had of a happier time with Ian, our last real vacation." She cried inwardly, "Our last vacation!" Getting more and more confused, she said aloud, "Maybe I would be just happier in a bigger place. A place I could fix up, where I could paint and create, have a nice room for Ian." On and on, she lamented. She knew if her own rambling was self-irritating, she must have been doing the same to him. She asked, "Michael am I making a mistake?"

Michael smiled, patted her shoulder, shook his head, and simply said, "No," He kept driving.

Seeing a sign for "Affordable New Homes" the house hunting team took a slight detour, and looked over the developing area. Though it was supposed to be near water, they could not see any signs of water from the road. Michael knew by Shannon's body language; they needed to move on. They got back in the car, and began heading back toward Cambridge. Shannon said, "I'm sorry Michael, I just need to feel right about the place, I bring Ian. She added, "Maybe Easton." Oh,

I just don't know! Maybe we should just head back home. I realize we should be closer to a hospital in case I need..." her voice trailed off. She was close to tears. Michael understood. He tried to assure her, and, at the same time, himself, they would find something. If not, maybe she would reconsider bringing Ian to Annapolis. At least there would be two of them caring for him; and it was certainly on the water. They had already discussed that option. Shannon agreed it was probably the best solution, but there seemed to be a driving force compelling her to stay in the area.

Prior to Ian's accident, Shannon would often tease Michael, "There's no peace in the Washington area." Possibly, now, seeing the advantage of being near Michael, she might reconsider the Annapolis option. They decided to take the old road toward Annapolis, instead of the freeway. Several farms, fields and small houses lined the roadway. It was a pleasant drive.

Suddenly, a young, slightly dark skinned girl with long flowing black hair was running alongside the car. She seemed to be pleading. Shannon actually saw a face, or rather; she thought she saw a face. She thought she saw tears falling on the young girl's cheeks. She ordered, "Michael, stop!"

Michael asked, "What?"

Shannon repeated, "Stop. Back up. There's a young girl out there. She seems to be in trouble."

Michael asked, "What girl?" His query made Shannon catch her breath for a moment. Remembering a familiar, sad, but frightening experience, she held her face in her hands. Michael thought she was just very tired. Not actually understanding why he was doing so, he obeyed Shannon's command and backed the car to a rugged signboard, by the road. He was not about to question this hard-headed beauty by his side.

A chilling recollection frightened Shannon. She realized they were in the same area that Ian had stopped their car, once before. She began thinking the previous encounter was a premonition of Ian's accident, or worse, a sign of his death.

For a moment, she thought this was another premonition. She was not sure it involved Ian any more. However, she was certain of one fact; she definitely saw the same young girl that she saw before. Something was wrong with her. She obviously needed help. Shannon wondered why she ran away as soon as they stopped the car. To be sure, Ian was ok; she quickly took out her cell phone and called home. Cora, the day nurse, answered the call, "Fitzpatrick's residence. Cora speaking."

Shannon said, "Hi Cora, I know I've already called you this morning, but is everything ok?"

Cora answered, "Everything is fine." Then she added, "The therapist was here this morning and everything looks good. Ian is well. Doctor Loren called. He wants Ian to have an MRI." She repeated, "Everything's fine. How are you?"

Shannon lied, "I'm fine." Her stomach ached. She felt as if she were going to a funeral, but at the same time, as if she had just fallen in love. She had that excited feeling, when 'he' looks at you for the first time.

Michael thought, "Intuition. Must be a woman thing." Snowflakes began falling over a sign nearby. Thinking a 'For Sale' sign was the reason they backed up, he asked, "Would you be wantin' to be seeing the sign, Luv?"

Shannon was beginning to calm, but was still in stress mode. She vaguely asked, "Huh?" Michael pointed to a very large neatly hand painted sign on a handmade signboard:

HOUSE
&
4 ACRES
4 SALE

There was a phone number listed. Shannon entered it in her cell phone, closed the phone and then looked again at the sign. It certainly was not a realtor's poster, but it was nicely printed. It looked as if an artist had used an old board to create a masterpiece. She stared at the sign, sighed, and stepped out of the car. She whispered, "I don't know, I don't know!"

Michael was confused as to why Shannon was reacting this way. To him, it was only a sign by the side of the road. He got out of the car and walked around to the other side. The property looked all right, but the field was somewhat overgrown.

A snowflake landed on Shannon's cheek. The thought of a snowstorm was all she needed. Michael said, "Just a field, Luv. Oh, there's a cute enough little cottage all right, but a big field. Looks kinda lonely."

Shannon looked around. She finally asked, "What cottage?" Shannon, being shorter than Michael, and the house being hidden by the high brush, had not seen it.

Michael pointed west, past the high grass. Shannon saw smoke coming out a chimney, but no house. She opened the car door, stepped up into the car, and looked westward to see the cottage. Looking at Michael for some sort of agreement or disagreement, she asked, "Shall we call?"

Michael shrugged his shoulders and smiled, but made no comment. He, thinking that particular cottage was a bad choice, and, in an attempt to dissuade her, said, "We can keep looking. We still have some time."

Shannon, still shaky from her very recent experience, held the cell phone so tightly in her hand her fingers were stinging. She was struggling with forces 'pro' and 'con' regarding the 'For Sale' sign. Suddenly she said, "Ok we'll call."

While waiting for a connection, she added, "The River is probably beyond the fields, maybe they'll have access." Shannon felt good about the area. Did she dare say that to Michael? She decided, "Not on your life! Take his son to this God-forsaken area? Hardly!"

A very nice, young female voice answered, "Reiner's Residence." Shannon said, "Hi, I'm here at a 'For Sale' sign by the road. Is this the party who has the house for sale?"

The voice answered, "Yes." She asked, "Would you like to see it? My husband is breaking for lunch. We can come right away, and show it to you. It's just around the bend in the road from the sign."

Shannon replied, "Yes, that would be great."

While waiting for the couple, Michael and Shannon sat in the car eating their 'time-saving' lunch, Michael smiled; thinking practical Shannon wanted to have as much time as possible for house hunting. He said, "Surely, they don't mean that little cottage." Shannon made no comment. Looking in the rear view mirror, and seeing a young couple get out of their car, she said, "What a sweet looking couple."

Michael teased, "Don't let appearances fool you, Luv. They could be real cut-throats y'know."

Shannon, who was always so positive about people, smiled and replied, "Oh, Michael!" She stepped out of the car and prepared to greet Bill and Patricia Reiner. Michael was happy just to see her smile.

After the introductions and a few amenities, Bill Reiner said, "We've been trying to keep the weeds down so's you could see the entire property. Didn't get to it before winter hit though. I thought I'd have time to do it before anyone actually wanted to see it." As they stood alongside the high brush on the shoulder of the road, he asked, "Do you want to follow us? The house is just up the road."

Shannon, almost afraid to see what it looked like, simply replied, "Sure." Almost expecting shutters hanging half off, but hoping she was wrong, she asked, "Is it empty?"

Bill said, "No it isn't. My wife's grandfather lives there alone. His wife died ten years ago."

As if Bill's statement was a painful one, Pat quietly said, "Yes, my Grandmother Arlene died two days before her eightieth birthday." After that one sentence, she clammed up.

Bill continued, "We're building closer to the bay. He will be living with us then. We're building a small annex for him. He'll have his own place and garden. We told him we needed more money. That's the only way we could convince him to go with us. We can't go off and leave him, and I just can't keep up

both properties, run my farm and take care of my family."
Shannon knew the feeling.

Trying to bring Pat back into the conversation, Shannon
asked, "Pat, how old is your grandfather?"

Pat's only answer was, "83, and very stubborn." Her
obvious reluctance to join in the conversation caused Shannon
to wonder if Bill Reiner was a bully. He seemed a nice enough
guy.

Bill was quick to add, "Yeah, old Chester Fargo is quite a
character, you'll see. You'll like him. I called him, to let him
know we might come over to his place." Pat smiled at his
statement. Pat's response to Bill's statement endeared Bill to
Shannon. She guessed he was not such a bully after all.

Shannon wondered why she had not noticed the house on
the way down the road. When they approached it, she knew
why. It had a slightly curved driveway. Though you could see
it from the road, and would see more if the field were mowed,
it actually sat around the bend, just as Bill said. As they drove
down the short lane, Shannon remembered the area. They
found out later, that Bill actually installed the sign while
Shannon and Michael were traveling around the Ocean City
area.

The pleasing sight of the house came into view. It was
extremely neat and well kept. However, it surprised her to see
a camping trailer setting at the back of the driveway. As she
stepped out of the car, and looked at it she thought,
"Interesting!" As if reading her mind Bill explained that Pat's
grandparents were campers. When they stopped because of the
wife's ill health, they kept the trailer. Chester could not bear to
part with it. He kept it in tip-top condition, covered with a tarp.

Bill said, "With the upcoming move it is coming in handy.
I parked it with the door close to the deck, so Chester could,
at his leisure, sort, and save what he wanted to take to his new
home. He was loading the trailer with small items, a little at a
time. By moving day, his treasured belongings will be packed
and ready to go."

Practical Michael thought it was a great idea. He teased Shannon, "Write that idea in your notebook, daughter."

Pat, finally joining the conversation, remarked, "He had better not try to do any loading if it continues to snow."

The house had a new wrap around deck. Thinking Bill looked like a capable handyman, rugged, like himself and Ian, Michael asked, "Did you build this deck Bill?"

Bill, touching the banister said, "Yes I did." He seemed happy to show off his handwork. He added, "and I made the railing myself."

Michael smiled and said, "Nice work." Shannon was relieved that Michael seemed to like the people. She hoped they liked the house.

Instead of stepping up on the deck, Bill pointed to the 'man-door' of the two-car garage, which sat to the left, at an 'L' angle to the house. As he opened the door, he asked them, "Would you like to see the garage first?"

Michael smiled and nodded to the affirmative. As he walked behind Shannon into the garage, he thought, "Guess we do."

Michael and Shannon were impressed with the neatness of the garage. They stood and chatted for a few minutes. Bill gestured for them to follow him. Thinking there was a possibility he was trying to butter them up before seeing the rest, Shannon was afraid of what the interior would look like, but the aroma of a wood-burning fireplace awoke her spirit. A warm, cozy feeling was beginning to encompass her.

As they were preparing to enter the interior door, Chester Fargo appeared in the doorway. He was a much younger looking man than Shannon thought he would be. He looked more like seventy than eighty-three, a tall, very attractive grey-haired gentleman with a gentle smile that encouraged Shannon to like him right away. Chester said, "I think I would have visitors enter through the main entrance, Bill."

The main entrance of the house was actually on the right side of the house. However, Chester seemed to be secretly happy that Bill showed them his workmanship in his wonderful garage. He put his hand on Bill's shoulders. Bill made the introductions. Michael complimented Chester on his handiwork, calling him Mr. Fargo. Chester smiled and said, "Chester will do just fine."

Michael appreciated the garage tour, but silently agreed with Chester about the main entrance. He smiled and thought, "Oh well. At least they did not try to sugar coat anything. They had a house for sale. Michael guessed the garage was the best of it, so they probably wanted to show it first.

Shannon was impressed with the mud/laundry room, with its own outside door between the garage and main area. She would soon discover the whole house was actually larger than it appeared from the road. Chester lead the way to the kitchen. As they entered, Bill, obviously proud of the older gent's talents, said, "Chester designed his home so every room has a view of the river.

Shannon began a question as she peered out of the kitchen area, "Oh, can you see the river from your house? The other homes we just looked at…"

Michael was deep in thought, and almost missed Shannon's excitement. He was thinking, "Hmm, she died ten years ago at the age of 80. He's just now eighty-three. Wow, the smart guy married an older woman. Nice going Chester." He respectfully smiled at his host.

Shannon stopped abruptly as she walked out of the kitchen area, realizing Bill's statement about the view. She silently exclaimed, "The view!" Now she understood her warm feeling. It was not just the wood burning fire, which was wonderful. It was the combination of Shannon's two favorite wonders of nature: fire and water.

Shannon, being comforted by Bill's word, '*View*' thought, "Oh, yes. It's the river!" She knew they had been close to it, though they never saw it. She remembered seeing a large body of water on the map, which fed from the Chesapeake. Apparently, they were concentrating so intently on the house as they were driving toward it, that they saw nothing beyond it. In addition, the trailer had blocked the view from the right, and the garage blocked it from the left. With the commotion of introductions and amenities as they entered the kitchen, she had not looked out the kitchen window. She exclaimed aloud, "What a view!"

Chester said, "It's the Choptank River."

Shannon answered, "Of course!" She thought to herself, "We've been following the river. This is the place. I know it!" Michael, also impressed with the scene in front of them, joined in Shannon's awe. He said, "What a view indeed!"

The house included three large bedrooms, two up, one down, the master. Every bedroom had a view of the river. In addition to the master bedroom on the main floor, were the kitchen that Shannon had just bolted out of, a walk-in pantry, a large dining/living room area, a small sewing room, a small den and an enclosed heated porch. The dining/living area had a cathedral ceiling and a balcony. It was the perfect house. She knew it. She began wondering, "What am I thinking? I would never be able to buy this place." She did not dare tell anyone how excited she was, or how her stomach was churning. It was almost as if she had to be there.

Shannon and Michael appreciated Chester Fargo's design. Chester explained, "I built each bedroom, up and down, in the front, facing the river. They're not too big, but 'M's' big enough for sleeping. Each one has a picture window. The hallway, bathrooms and the big closets are on the road side. After our children were not living here, we used the rooms for guest. We wanted everybody who stayed with us to have a tranquil night sleep with a water view. My idea was almost my 'undoin', though. Folk would come to visit and never want to leave. I practically had to adopt my guests." His statement got a chuckle from everyone.

Michael especially loved Chester's old Eastern Shore Colloquialism. He would later find out 'M' was an old Eastern Shore word for 'they', they are, 'they're' or 'those are'.

Standing in one of the upstairs bedrooms, looking across the river, Shannon began to love the house even more. She was going to hate to leave it, but knew it would be way out of her price range if she wanted to pay cash. It was bad enough that she was making other decisions without the benefit of Ian's council. Her mind was racing, "Hmm, Michael's money?"

CHAPTER NINE
Is This Home?

When the group were standing on the deck facing the river, Chester pointed to a small cottage and said, "I never had need for a studio. I had my den." Referring to his late wife, he added, "It was her idea. I built it after listening to her nag about it. She knew what I needed more than I did. I spent most of my days in there dabbling in my painting and such. I don't use it much anymore."

Shannon whispered, "Studio? Did he say studio?" That did it! She had to have that house. She almost knew it was much more than she could afford, even if she used all their savings. Nevertheless, her mind was whirling as she thought, "Wonder if Michael would like to be a co-owner?" With her stomach tightening, she braced herself for the asking price and inquired, "How much are you asking."

Chester answered, "Three hundred thousand, if you just want the house, and the half-acre west, another hundred thousand if you want the other two acres." With his Eastern Shore draw, he added, "Ye should really take that piece, though." Pointing to the location of the 'For Sale' sign, he continued, "If I sell it to somebody else, they'll be building close to you. That's for sure." He looked proud and pleased with himself that he could still negotiate his own deals.

Putting his arm on Bill's shoulder, Chester continued, "The kids need more money than they have. Don't want them going into debt if I can help it." He went on, "They have two little ones, need more room. They've built me a little house hooked onto it so's it'll be all right." He had Michael's positive attitude.

Shannon was not sure she heard right. She asked, "Three and a half acres?"

Chester corrected her. "The house sits on one and a half acre. There is a half-acre to the west of the house, and two acres to the east. Four acres, four-hundred thousand bucks. That's the deal, take it or leave it."

Yvonne Dorsey

An excited Shannon declared, "I'll take it." She was not going to take a chance on someone else coming along and buying 'her' house. Michael did a double take. Shannon asked Pat, "When will your house be finished?"

Pat, finally joining the conversation, and with her words almost sounded like a little ditty, answered, "It is built, we just need to fine finish, and furnish it."

A rare occurrence happened. Michael was speechless. Bill, adding to Pat's statement, said, "Should be done in a month or so if the weather holds out."

Shannon, hoping to could work out the details that day and get back to Ian, explained her circumstances. Her predicament emotionally moved the Marylanders. They agreed to work out the details that afternoon. Shannon said she would pay cash. They were shocked. Chester liked her right away. He felt good about her living in the home his love built. Within two hours, the transfer worked out to everyone's satisfaction.

Michael was happy for the short drive, from eastern Annapolis. He teased that it was his presence, and the luck of the Irish, that brought Shannon to the house. Bill related the facts of Chester's decision on the method he would sell his dream house. Shannon smiled at Chester, who seemed pleased with the enthusiasm of the young man.

Chester knew that, if he went through a realtor and took more time, he could get more money. He had already decided he would do the advertising and selling. He would stay within the law, but he just wanted to sell his house the old-fashioned way. 'Shake a hand'. 'Pay the man'. 'Pass the deed'.

He painted a simple sign. As Bill hammered it in the ground, beside the road, Chester said, "Good enough." He promised that if he did not sell the property in a month he would list it more properly (by modern standards) and would set a higher asking price. Bill and Pat thought Chester was dreaming that the right person would just drive by.

Shannon thought this deal was proper enough and knew she was the 'right person'. She shook hands with Chester, as did Michael. Being aware the old-fashioned Chester would prefer having a check in his hand, than one in the mail, she wrote a check for the full asking price. Aware of Chester's cautious nature, she worked out a deal. She would give Michael permission to act as her agent, and give the check to him to hold. As soon as she got home, she would transfer the money into her checking account. By an agreed date, Michael would hand-deliver the check to Chester. Chester would sign the house over to Shannon through Michael.

Trying to assure the older gent she would come through with the money, Shannon smiled, and said to him, "You agree not to show or sell the house until the agreed date. Our deal is still valid until then, ok?" Chester agreed. He felt that Shannon was an honest person.

Actually, Shannon was not feeling very honest. She knew the property was worth much more than the amount they had just negotiated, and that Bill and Pat knew it. They must have wanted a fast sell. They got it in Shannon Marie D'Arcy Fitzpatrick.

Remembering Ian, Shannon suddenly felt a chill going up her back. She thought, "He's going to kill me. Should I have waited? Is it right to decide this without him?" For a moment she wondered, "Should I back out of this deal?" However, just as quickly, she thought, "Nope. It is too late. The deal is made. If needed, we can always sell it for a profit. I'll make it right with him later." She was Ian's caretaker, and had to do whatever she needed to do to care for him. Final decision!

Michael's head was spinning. He asked himself, "Did she just buy a house so quickly? The girl's got guts." He had always admired his daughter-in-law, but that day he had complete respect for her ability to take charge.

Chester wanted to show Michael and Shannon the dock and cottage before they left. It looked as if the house sat about

Yvonne Dorsey

four hundred feet from the river, and was at a very nice elevation, with the studio cottage slightly closer to the water, but still at a nice elevation. Shannon was anxious to see the little cottage. They walked down toward the river. Snow slightly covered the yard. The air was brisk, but very inviting. It was a pleasant day. The river looked splendid. Even considering the re-occurring feeling of sadness and fright at the area where the road curved, Shannon was experiencing peace, a feeling she had not come close to having since Ian's accident.

The men were standing on the dock, looking over the river, and engaged in conversation. Pat offered to show Shannon the inside of the cottage. Once inside, Shannon was in love. Looking out of the window to the river, she remarked, "What a delightful place to work." Pat agreed. She said that her grandfather spent many happy hours there.

The women started a slow walk up toward the house. Shannon felt that Pat was uncomfortable about something. She decided to draw her into conversation and, maybe ease her tension, "Pat, this is a lovely home. I'm surprised you and Bill didn't just add on and live here. Do you just want to move closer to the bay?"

Pat's only answer was, "Yes." Then, obviously trying to change the subject, she asked, "Shannon do you think you'll build on the other three acres?"

Shannon replied, "I don't know." She added, "We'll probably clear it and decide later, after my husband..." She cleared her throat. Nodding toward the house, she asked Pat, "Do you think it's haunted?"

A startled Pat turned, looked as if Shannon had just exposed a deep, dark secret and answered, "No!" Then she asked, "What made you ask that?"

Shannon answered, "I believe it might be." She added, "Or possibly somewhere close by is, but it doesn't bother me. I think I'm supposed to be here." She asked Pat, "Did your grandmother think it was haunted?" Pat answered, "No. She never thought the house was haunted." As a hesitating

90

afterthought, she added, "But, maybe the area around it." Pointing in the direction of the 'For Sale' sign by the road, she added, "Right about over there." Looking over to the field, she continued, "Grandmother Arlene always felt that something was wrong. She said every time she walked up the road from the Reiner's farm she felt sad, and just knew it was haunted, but no harm ever came to her. After a while, she just accepted it. However, when she got older she hated walking up the road."

Shannon continued her questioning, "Did your grandfather think it was haunted?"

Pat answered, "No, he thought my grandmother had a great imagination." Pat was sorry she had started talking about the haunting, but it felt so good, finally being able to speak of it.

Shannon continued, "Pat, may I ask you something? Do you ever get the feeling when you're in that area?" They both looked over to where Pat had pointed.

Pat, hesitating to answer, finally replied, "Yes, but not when I was a child. It only started one summer while I was visiting my grandparents, when I began dating Bill. I thought some evil force did not want me here. I told Grandma Arlene about it. That's when she told me about her experiences. It seems only a few women she knew of ever mentioned the 'haunting' experience." There, she said it! It seemed as if her own words had lifted a giant weight from her shoulders.

Shannon echoed Pat's description, "Haunting!" Then continuing, she said, "Maybe more women than you know have had a similar experience and never mentioned it. Was that why you were so quiet when we first met?"

Pat replied, "Yes."

Shannon asked, "Did Bill ever mention any feelings he had when he was there?"

Pat answered, "No, he thinks I'm nuts when I tell him about it. I just don't mention it anymore. I think he was apprehensive about me being alone with you, afraid I would say something about the haunting, and discourage you."

As the conversation continued, Pat began feeling bad about Shannon buying the house, wondering if they had tricked her, and if she should demand her grandfather tear up the signed contract. She was more than surprised when Shannon exclaimed, "This is great! Now I have something to work with, I'll figure it out." She smiled at Pat and said, "It'll be all right. I promise to take great care of your family's home." Shannon gave Pat a wonderfully bright smile. Pat's eyes lit up as if she had just received a wonderful gift. She had, but she would not realize it until much later.

Shannon's mind was awhirl. She remembered Ian thought she was having a weird moment and a bad dream when they were riding past the area. He drove right past it and felt nothing. Neither did Michael. Chester and Bill both thought their wives were just imagining things. She thought, "Hmm... a few chosen women, huh? I can't wait to get back here and do some investigating." She repeated aloud, "Hmm, a few chosen women!" Though the whole idea was disturbing, Shannon actually felt honored to be included. They walked in silence for a couple of minutes. Pat seemed to be uncomfortable. Shannon repeated her words of assurance, "It'll be all right Pat." She smiled and asked her, "Will you come to visit me when we move in?"

Pat answered, "Sure! You bet I will." She was more than happy with her new special friend with whom she had already shared a '**secret**'. As if needing further reassurance, she asked, "Shannon, do you think there is a haunting?"

Shannon answered, "Sure I do." Then, she added, "But it seems only women feel it. Maybe men are too dense. We must be special." They both laughed.

By the time the young women reached the deck, the men were leaning over the banister, talking. They visited for a few more minutes. Michael and Shannon said their good-byes, and prepared to leave. As Michael turned the car around to exit the driveway, Shannon waved good-bye to her new friends. She wondered if Chester was crying on the inside, but smiling on the outside. She voiced her concern to Michael. Michael answered, "Sure he is, but not to worry, Luv. He'll be around from time to time. That's for sure. We talked."

Shannon smiled and said, "Yeah, you're right. He will be around. I like him; and I can guarantee you talked."

For the first few minutes of the trip back to Annapolis, Michael seemed to be in a contemplative mood. Just as Shannon began resting her eyes, he announced, "That Chester sure is something."

The sudden jump in conversation startled Shannon. She opened her eyes, looked at him and simply agreed, "Yes, he surely is."

Michael, not even realizing Shannon's languid state, went on, "I thought he was originally from this area, the way he talks about it, but he was born on the far eastern parts, in Ocean City. He was a commercial fisherman down there, he was. Worked his way through college catching fish. Imagine that, fishing for college."

Shannon, forced awake, laughed and added, "Imagine that."

Michael continued, "Chester told me that Bill and Pat wanted to live on the Chesapeake Bay. When he and Pat made the announcement, that they were moving from the homestead, Bill's cousin, Sue and her husband, Rob, who had been living with Sue's mother, Martha, bought the house. They both worked out of the area, but would still live on the family farm. Aunt Martha was very content indeed! Her daughter and son-in-law would still be nearby. Her son, Bud, partners with Bill, in the farming business, would still be coming for lunch every workday. Bud lived on Martha's portion of the farmland.

When Bill's father passed away, Bill inherited his father's share of the farm and inherited the home, with the stipulation that Bill's mother, Ruth, could continue to live with him. Bill and Pat wanted her to stay with them anyway, and especially hoped she would love the new home they were building."

Shannon was amused at height of excitement in her father-in-law's voice as he relayed information about her future neighbors. He loved history, anyone's. Michael continued, "Bill had originally been concerned his mom would not be happy with the move; she was happy to be going back to her old home area, the Chesapeake Bay.

Pat was very close to her grandparents, Chester and Arlene Fargo. After her grandmother Arlene died, her grandfather depended on her and Bill for emotional and physical support. Her mother, Marie, Chester's daughter, tried to convince Chester to live with her and her husband in Baltimore. He declined. He visits her often."

Michael said, "There's some interesting folk living in the area. Chester says you will get to love them as neighbors and friends. He sure is something, that Chester. I liked him right away, didn't you, Shannon?"

Shannon answered, "Yes I did, Michael, and I think you are also 'something.' He grinned, looking pleased at himself for the remembrance of Chester's story. Shannon was always amazed at his acute memory and attention to details. She guessed that was what made him a great ambassador.

The next morning, with the house hunting over, Shannon boarded a plane for home and Ian. As she tucked her carry-on bag into the baggage compartment, she prayed, "God, please let this be right. Let Ian understand," She closed her eyes and slept the entire flight, awaking as the plane landed.

CHAPTER TEN
Going to the River

Kim, with her 'pep talk' well rehearsed, was waiting by the baggage claim. Expecting a downtrodden Shannon, she was more than shocked to hear Shannon's bubbly voice, "Hey, Kim, you're here already. We're early. I was prepared to wait. This is great. Boy, have I got things to tell you."

Kim was slightly disappointed that Shannon was apparently fine and not in need of cheering. On the way home, Shannon shared her news. Kim fought back tears as she realized her best friend was actually moving away.

Shannon was so excited about her new home that she actually seemed insensitive to Kim's feelings. Realizing that, she quickly apologized, "Oh, Kim, I'm sorry. I am really going to miss you. Look at it this way. You and Keith will have a place to 'get away'. We will always be good friends. Please forgive me for leaving. Maybe it will only be for a while, I don't know, but I do know I need your friendship wherever I am. I desperately need some peace in my life. I have it when I'm on the water. I need you to please support me in this, will you?"

Kim dried her tears and said, "I'll always be there for you Shannon, you know that. If you think it's the right thing, it's good enough for me. What the heck, we'll have free lodging on Maryland's Eastern Shore. Who can complain about free lodging, Right?"

Shannon had passed through one hurdle with Kim. She still had to break the news to her family, friends and to her wonderful landlords/friends.

Kim dealt with the shock of Shannon's new plan. They spent the drive home discussing Ian, and the successful "nursing experience."

January and all of **February** were busy months. There was much to do. Shannon tearfully gave notice to her landlords, finished her free-lance jobs and said good-bye to family and friends, with a promise to invite them to her new home. She spent the majority of her time preparing to move Ian and his equipment, deciding not to sell anything. They would sell or save everything together, according to their plan. She could even think 'Plan' again. She was not sure it would ever become a reality, but it was her anchor. The MRI proved Ian to be in good condition. Doctor Loren was confident that Ian was able to make the trip by ambulance.

Shannon needed to go back to Maryland once more before the final move. She wanted to simplify moving day by setting up the kitchen as much as possible. In addition, she needed to interview the nurse Michael had 'found'. He planned to bring the two women together while Shannon was in Maryland. Shannon hoped they would be compatible. She decided she would simply trust Michael. Kim decided to take a vacation week and go with her.

Cora, the regular day nurse, agreed to come two hours early to relieve the night nurse Shannon hired for the week. Keith promised to come by each day after work, and assist in any way he could. Shannon and Kim planned to return before the following weekend. Michael had the Maryland utilities changed to Shannon's name.

Very early Sunday morning Keith and Kim arrived at the apartment. Though Shannon felt awkward leaving Ian, she was secretly thrilled to get away to the river. She felt guilty even thinking those thoughts, but soon, she and Kim were in the car, beginning their journey to Maryland. Shannon took her journal, the log of her daily life. As she drove the car away, she nervously looked through the rear view window, and silently prayed her constant prayer, "Lord, please let this be right."

The drive to Maryland went smoothly. Shannon felt peaceful about her new plans. Kim was apprehensive, but supportive. The weather for the week was favorable. As they approached the Bay Bridge leading to the Eastern Shore, Shannon said, "Good week for the Eastern Shore." The sight of the water always triggered a 'catch breath.' That day was no exception.

Kim's only reply was, "It's a beautiful day all right." She secretly thought the Long Island Sound was just as beautiful. Even when Shannon pulled into the driveway, Kim simply said, "Oh, it's nice."

Shannon did not know how to take Kim's reaction, but she had not appreciated the beauty of the house at first, so she was not too concerned. However, she had already fallen in love with the place. It was going to be her home, so she was a little hurt. She thought, "It's…nice? Just…it's nice? She, for sure, does not like it. Oh no, is this like the old forties movie 'The Enchanted Cottage' where Robert Young and Dorothy McGuire saw beauty in each other when they were in the enchanted cottage, that no one else could see?"

Shannon reasoned that Michael loved the house also, so it must be ok. Realizing the absurd 'self' volley of questions and answers, she just smiled at her friend and parked the car in the driveway. Locating the hidden key, she made sure they entered through the main entrance. She wanted Kim to see the beauty of the river right away. Kim did see it. It was obvious she was impressed with the beautiful winter scene. Shannon could tell Pat had tried to leave everything as nice as possible. Bill had even stacked plenty of firewood on the hearth.

Shannon's plan was to get the unpacking and cleaning finished as quickly as possible, enjoy a nice fire each evening and have some time to explore the area and share her new home with Kim. The past eighteen months had been a strain on both of them. They needed a break. That week was it.

Monday: As Kim was empting a box in the kitchen, she thought to herself, "This place is wonderful and tranquil, but I'm just not sure what she hopes to accomplish, moving here." The security of New York City and New Jersey seemed so far away. She was sad for Shannon and silently wondered, "What is she thinking?" She kept her thoughts to herself, and kept busy with the task of getting Shannon settled. They spent the day cleaning an already clean house, putting away food items, and squeezing in a little 'river watching'.

By early evening, the young women were exhausted. The cool March air was refreshing after a hard day's work. They stood on the deck and enjoyed a glass of wine. The moon graced the river.

Shannon, speaking as if she had just made a decision, said, "Tomorrow, we'll just clean up our clutter and relax. It will do until we move in. Wednesday, we'll do some sightseeing. Thursday, Michael will be here with the nurse he found. I suppose I will just have to trust his idea." It was obvious to Kim that making positive productive plans was beneficial for Shannon.

The area in front of the fireplace was the perfect place for a dining and sleeping area. They unrolled their sleeping bags, relaxed and ate their dinner. As they sat by the fire, Kim realized Shannon was in a very peaceful state. She noticed a difference in the tone of her voice, as they talked. Her thoughts wandered to a conversation the two had earlier in the day when they were having lunch at a very small table on the enclosed heated porch. A little table set was the only furniture in the house. They had previously discussed moving it into the living room, but decided to reserve it for breakfast and lunch. They could enjoy the river view with their daylight meals. Kim remembered watching Shannon caress it during lunch. She recalled her words. Referring to her new friend, Chester Fargo, Shannon had said,

"He and his wife loved their home. He built this house and made this table set. He said she loved to sit here on the porch and work on puzzles, or just relax in her recliner. She would knit and watch the river for hours. He must have really loved his wife, the way he talks about her." Her voice was mellow, as if she were already a kindred spirit with the older gentleman. As she caressed the table, she said, "It is a beautiful table. I

don't know why he left it."

An appreciative Kim watched Shannon's tired hand move over the table. She smiled, got up, gave her friend a long hug and a gentle pat on the back, and said, "I know why."

The sound and aroma of burning wood brought Kim out of her musing, and back to their fireside conversation. A relaxed Kim gently told Shannon, "It is lovely here, Shannon. I mean the whole package." Then, she added, "Especially the river view. I love it, and I know Ian will love it too." Kim's words gently pleased Shannon.

Tuesday: The time went by so quickly. The two women had been working steadily. They were tired, but their mood was much lighter than when they first arrived. They were more than ready to quit for the day. It was the end of their second workday. They settled down to an early dinner.

Kim was becoming to have peace with Shannon's decision to move to the river. She was impressed that Shannon could build a fire. When she remarked about the fact, Shannon, as she methodically stoked the logs, said, "Kally taught me. Whenever I smell a wood burning fire, I think of her." Shannon's eyes began tearing. Trying to dismiss the feeling, she picked up the wine bottle and asked, "More wine?" Kim nodded the affirmative.

As Shannon poured the wine, Kim asked, "Shannon, why do you refer to you mom as Kally?"

Shannon answered, "The sound of her name keeps her real to me." She looked deep into the fire. As if a floodgate had opened, and, in spite of threatening tears, Shannon continued her reminiscence of Kally, "I called her Mom when I was little. After my Dad died, Kally become more than my total support. She was my friend. I would never have survived, nor had any ambition without her. She was, and still is, my saint." Shannon paused for a moment, and then added, "I wish you could have met her, Kim. She would have liked you and you would have liked her."

Taking a sip of wine, Shannon continued, "When Kally died, I thought my world would just stop. I was still in high school. I felt so alone. I wanted to do nothing except lie around all day wallowing in self-pity. Uncle Brian and Aunt Louise helped me a lot, but I felt dry, just 'plain ole', dry. They reminded me of my promise to Kally, to continue my education and to grow as a person. Finally. I was able to keep my promise by going to college. Thank God I did. I met Ian. Mom sure knew what she was doing. I always believed she sent Ian to me."

Kim thought it strange the way Shannon's description of Kally D'Arcy changed often, sometimes in the same paragraph, from Mom to Kally, then back to 'Mom' again.

Wednesday: The sightseeing was off the planned schedule because of rain. Shannon wished Michael were coming that day, so she could get the interview over with, and go home to Ian.

As if he knew Shannon needed a 'rainy day' pick-me-up, Chester Fargo called. He asked if it would be a good day for him and Pat to come by with a hot meal. Having nothing else to do until Thursday, and considering the cold rain and hot meal, it was indeed, a good time.

Chester and Pat brought in two folding chairs from the cottage; the four of them were able to sit around the little table on the enclosed porch.

Even with the pouring rain, the river was magnificent. The glowing fireplace in view through the picture window, made it very cozy. After lunch, Pat and Kim carried the dishes to the kitchen, and stayed there to make coffee. Shannon and Chester remained in conversation. Shannon caressed the table, and said to her new friend, "Chester, you left your table."

As naturally as Shannon had done, Chester also caressed the little table, and replied, "It wasn't my table. It was hers.

Figured you would use it more than I would. I like my old maple table, like to spread my newspapers out, you know?"

Shannon knew Chester's memories of the little table were special to him; he must have regarded her as a very special friend to be able to give it away so freely. She got up, walked around to his side of the table and kissed him on his forehead. She whispered, "Thank you." He smiled. The two of them needed few words. Later, watching the visitors leave the driveway, Shannon enjoyed a warm feeling of 'family'.

The rain stopped; the sky promised a beautiful Thursday. Kim said she understood why Shannon spoke so kindly about Chester. He was a very special gentleman. Pat was also impressive as a friend. She felt more positive about Shannon's new home. They spent the evening as previous, with a glass of wine and relaxing conversation by the fire.

Shannon was awake long after Kim fell asleep. As she watched the dancing flames, and occasional twinkle of stars through the porch windows, she remembered her phone conversation with Michael:

An excited Michael had told her of his idea of bringing a couple to help her, an Irish couple needing employment. Shannon had almost dropped the phone. Instead, she had blurted out, "A couple? Michael, I can't afford a couple. I'm even nervous about employing a full time, live in nurse, let alone a couple! The insurance will only pay for a day and an evening nurse. A live in nurse is way out of my league. A couple? I can't afford to pay an extra person."

Michael said he could not stand the thoughts of her being 'out there' all alone. True, she would have a nurse during the day and part of the evening, but not overnight. He has asked, "What would you do in case of an emergency? Just you and a nurse is not enough, Shannon. If there were a problem, it would probably take the two of you to care for Ian. Who would call for help? In addition, a man could certainly turn and move Ian better. Shannon, you are going to destroy your back, not to mention the back of a nurse doing such hard work, day after day. A live-in nurse and a man working around the place is the only true answer to our situation."

"Our situation." he had said, "our situation." His words caused Shannon to cry.

Michael said the nurse would take complete care of Ian, plus his laundry and nutrition. Her husband would work in the capacity of a handyman. Michael would pay him a small salary. He had thought the studio looked like a proper cottage for them, and hoped he could convince Shannon to give it up as a painting studio, only temporarily, just until Ian awoke. It grieved him every time he thought about his son's condition, but Shannon was his 'daughter' and he was going to take care of her as well.

Michael's fatherly involvement in her dilemma heartened Shannon. A couple was a very good solution, but she wondered how Michael pulled off the deal. She was sure the woman was a very qualified nurse. He certainly had an interest in Ian's welfare and knew he would not have hired her if she were not. Shannon wondered, "Why is she taking this job?"

Michael felt that, with some relief, Shannon could spend more time on her own projects, and still care for Ian. Actually, his mind was processing the idea as soon as Shannon shook hands with Chester Fargo. He knew Shannon would need help taking care of his son and their new home. Just as Shannon got her idea like a bolt of lightning, so did Michael. He knew the answer, and he thought he just might know the right couple.

A small crackle of firewood giving way to a flame brought Shannon back to the reality of her new surroundings. Trying to relax, and give in to sleep, she fluffed her pillow, buried her face in it, and whispered gently, "Sleep Clouds take me. I'm yours!" Her words waning, she finally slept.

Thursday: Michael, prompt as usual, arrived at 10:00 a.m. with the young couple, Sean and his wife, Kaitlin Rose. They were 'very Irish', complete with a thick brogue and all. "Well, hmm," thought Shannon. After all the amenities, Shannon showed them around her home. To her surprise, she felt as saved by them as she always did by Michael. She needed help, and she knew it. Sean was a farmer, as he put it. Michael said Sean's lifetime was about agriculture. He was involved in youth projects as a lad and teen; and had just completed a three-year college course in Ireland. Using the word, "Farmer" was humbling. He wanted to study in America.

Kaitlin Rose was a very qualified nurse, having attended nursing school in America as well as in Ireland. Shannon no longer wondered why Kaitlin Rose, obviously over qualified, would take such a job. She knew of a Kaitlin Rose, and decided she would verify her supposition later.

Over coffee and toasted week old coffeecake, the group agreed on the 'new plan'. Michael would move the couple in before Shannon and Ian arrived. Everyone seemed to be in accord with the logistics Michael had drafted. Shannon was relieved he had taken control.

The group continued their meeting over lunch at the Inn where Michael and Shannon stayed earlier in the year, purchased fresh pastry and then concluded their visit back at the new home. Shannon headed to the kitchen to make coffee. She asked her father-in-law, "Would you help me, Michael?"

Michael mischievously answering "Right behind ya, Luv," followed her to the kitchen.

Away from the chatter, Shannon asked, "How was your trip, Michael?"

Michael asked, "Trip?"

Shannon smiled and tapped at his shoulder. "Yes, your trip to Ireland. You handpicked these people and I know it. I think

I know who they are."

Michael smiled and sheepishly whispered, "Well, I guess I shouldn't have tried to fool the likes of you, Shannon Fitzpatrick." He went on, "Kaitlin Rose is actually my cousin, twice removed, Ian's third." Shannon nodded.

Michael continued, "I was talking to my very own first cousin, Elizabeth, in Ireland about Ian's condition, and the situation you were in. She merely mentioned her Kaitlin Rose, my wife's namesake, being born just before Ian, wanted to come to America to work for a while. Her hubby would have to find work as well so he could attend to his studies." Michael, qualifying Sean's participation, said, "He will study only part-time and at home for now, Shannon."

Michael, continuing his presentation, said, "After Ian is…you know…when you don't need as much help, Sean and Kaitlin Rose will get their own apartment closer to a city and he will begin attending classes. Kaitlin Rose could then work at a large hospital near him. What could a body do, but to offer transportation over here just for a wee trial period? Not to worry now, Shannon. Not to worry."

Michael seemed to have all details covered. Shannon decided to trust him. He, feeling good enough to tease, continued, "Besides, they're cousins to you now, Shannon. They are family. Families help families. And didn't ye say your own great-grandmother was Rosie Fitzpatrick. Why, they could be your cousins too."

Shannon thought, "Good grief, I could be married to my own cousin." She did not need to hear that, but being satisfied Michael knew best, she suggested they re-join the group. While they enjoyed their dessert and coffee on the enclosed porch, Sean's eyes were flitting from area to area. It was obvious to Shannon that he was excited by the challenge of working on the property.

Soon, Michael and the cousins departed, leaving Shannon feeling a bit more secure in her new settlement.

A New Plan was under way!

Friday: Kim awoke early to the welcome aroma of coffee. She thought, "Thank God for automation!" Surprisingly, Shannon was sleeping soundly. Settling issues was definitely proving beneficial. She soon awoke. Their day began afresh.

After breakfast, they prepared the car for their return journey. The air seemed fresh and clear. They decided to take their Wednesday's canceled walk. They walked down to the river. Then, Shannon led the way to the road. Walking down the road, Kim asked, "Do you think you'll be lonely here, Shannon?"

Shannon answered, "It will be different here, for sure. I will miss you and everyone, but I don't think I will be too lonely. I'll be busy. Then, of course, the cousins will be here." After about twenty minutes, they turned direction and headed back.

Kim, being worried about her friend, began to say, "I was thinking maybe Keith and I would come down during Easter or maybe spend our vaca...! She suddenly stopped walking, turned and looked at Shannon, muttering, "Oh my God, something's wrong!"

Though she had called Keith a few minutes prior, Kim nervously fumbled for her cell phone and called him again. Shannon called the nurse. All was well. However, Kim felt shaky for the entire walk home.

Later, on the drive home, she apologized to Shannon for not believing her earlier experience.

A few weeks later was finally, moving day. Keith picked up Michael at the airport. Kim and the relatives helped Shannon with the last minute moving details. Soon, it was time to leave. While everyone was outside, watching the transport team prepare Ian for his journey, a bittersweet Shannon stood alone, crying in the doorway of her home. Her family and friends all promised to visit. She doubted if anyone, besides Kim, Keith and her aunt and uncle, would actually come. Michael had arranged plenty of time to facilitate the move.

Saying good-bye to the Turners, whose home she and Ian had shared, was a sad moment. John stroked Ian's hand as a father caressing a son. Watching the older couple's sad faces, Shannon realized how lucky she and Ian had been to have them in their lives. They promised to keep in touch. She hoped they would, but was sad that it might be the last time she would ever see them.

As Ian was being lifted into the ambulance, and seeing the sadness in the older couple's faces, Shannon said to Michael, "Poor Ian never got the chance to say good-bye to them."

Michael said, "Maybe he is saying it right now, Luv."

Shannon touched her father-in-law's arm and replied, "Yeah, maybe."

Shannon had a moment of doubt as she watched the Ambulance Personnel secure Ian and his equipment. Michael Put his hand on her shoulder and advised, "Trust Ian to God and the transport team. They know what they are doing." Shannon nodded.

Michael and Keith had attached Shannon's car to the hitch of the rental truck. Shannon tucked their snack bags in the van, and after several hugs and many, many tears, they were off to Maryland.

CHAPTER ELEVEN
Leaving Home, Finding Home

The trip to Maryland, unlike the previous one, seemed to take forever. Following the ambulance was a slow process and very nerve wrecking, but Shannon wanted to be as close to Ian as possible. She called Sean when they were nearing the area. As the moving team arrived at the new homestead, Sean and Kaitlin Rose were waiting at the door.

The readied coffee, glowing fireplace, and a wonderful aroma of homemade stew gave a promise of homey comfort. Even with a lack of furniture, the ambience was one of warmth and invitation.

Per Shannon's request, Michael had a security system installed in Ian and Shannon's room, with monitors in each room, for viewing during daylight hours. In order to use the fireplace and because of Ian's oxygen usage, the bedroom door would remain closed. In addition, and per Shannon's request, Michael had prepared a room for himself. The cousins settled in an upstairs room until the cottage could be refurbished as a more suitable private dwelling. The den was Shannon' getaway and reading room.

The ambulance attendants quickly secured Ian in the new hospital bed. Doctor Loren, Ian's New Jersey doctor, had already notified a colleague to expect a call from Shannon regarding Ian's schedule. Shannon had done so. Doctor Craig Wallace, who had already received Ian's complete history, arrived shortly and was immediately in charge. He and Shannon had developed a patient/care/phone relationship and he had forwarded preliminary written instructions to Kaitlin Rose. She was very quickly attending to Ian.

Sean, Michael and Shannon unloaded and arranged the furniture. The boxes were quickly unpacked and the meager belongings put away. Shannon felt guilty, not tending to her husband, but knowing Kaitlin Rose was so capable was comforting. As she set the table for dinner, Shannon teased,

"Sean, I bet you were happy to see such a small amount of furniture to carry in."

Sean replied, "Surprised was more like it." He added in his thick Irish brogue, "I was 'a thinkin' we would be the entire night unloadin."

Shannon was afraid she seemed too callous. Michael had already had a long talk with the cousins. They admired her for what she was trying to do, and were more than happy to be a part of Ian's recovery. Kaitlin Rose was hard pressed to come out of Ian's room. Watching her, Shannon felt completely at ease about Ian's care.

Later, as she sat by Ian's bedside, Shannon said, "Well Ian, here we are partner, in our paradise. All you have to do is to awaken. Please Ian, wake up. Come back to me" Then she added, "And when you do, don't be mad." She settled down for the first night, in their own home, in her twin bed, next to Ian's hospital bed, with a promise to call Kaitlin Rose if she needed her, no matter the hour.

Michael stayed for a few days, and then headed back to Washington in time for his Monday morning meeting. The landscaping firm he hired was busy clearing the adjoining field. Shannon did not fight him on the matter. She was concerned about spending so much money.

When the workers cleared the field, the three cousins were thrilled to see a huge pile of rocks seemingly appear at the bend of the river. Shannon was thrilled that she could see more of the river. Kaitlin Rose remarked, "Oh my, that rock looks like a giant bird or even an angel. That's it. It is your very own guardian angel watching over your property." Sean and Shannon laughed at her theory. The three cousins soon adapted to their new schedules.

April: The new residents of Chester's 'Creation' were not prepared for the wonders they experienced in the awakening of spring, on their little portion of the Choptank River. Shannon felt every seed catalog she had ever drooled over, had suddenly come alive in front of her very own eyes. She remembered a poem on a heart shaped plaque someone had once given her:

"Who plants a seed beneath the sod,
Then waits to see, believes in God."
'Author unknown'

When Shannon was sharing this joy with Chester one day. She complimented him on the awesome grandeur he had created. He said it was not his creation. It was Arlene's. He merely kept it alive for her. He knew Shannon would try to do the same for him. Clever man, that Chester! He knew just what to say. Shannon knew he was setting her up to take extra special care of 'his home'. She pledged to keep Arlene's dream alive.

Over the spring months, Sean and Chester dug many bulbs, re-planted and took some to Bill's new home, leaving plenty for Shannon. Chester guided Sean to the best selections of flowers and vegetables for the locale. Sean was in his glory, working on the property. With the river's night mist, the buds, greens and blooms flourished. Chester loved to help Sean from time to time. Shannon felt she was certainly the recipient of their joy.

The earth welcomed the planting; the garden promised a wonderful fall harvest. Everyone had their own agenda and went about their own daily tasks. It was the sixth change of season Shannon spent without sharing the news of the day with Ian.

Shannon and Kaitlin Rose eventually developed a good working relationship. Ian's physical therapist came three days a week, with Kaitlin Rose doing gentle massage on alternate days, being careful not to over work Ian's motionless body. Shannon felt good about the quality of care Ian was receiving. She was glad she quit her full-time job to care for him. She secured artwork to do at home to generate a small income.

May: One afternoon, as Shannon walked toward the garage

door to go on some errands; she called out to Sean, "I'll be back in about two hours."

CHAPTER TWELVE
Do I Still Love?

When Shannon stepped into the beautiful garage, she began thinking about Chester and Arlene Fargo. Getting into the car, she wondered about the many times they must have walked through the garage to go shopping, to the movies, or to visit the 'kids' (referring to Bill and Pat). A loving warmth came over her. She remembered the first time she met Chester, in the doorway of the garage. She remembered his countenance when he spoke of his Arlene. Suddenly, she remembered, she did not say good-bye to Ian. She questioned, "Oh God am I falling out of love with him?" Everything she did seemed so automatic and functional. Often, she thought that she might as well be running a home health care business, and that, Ian's care, and the property, was becoming her life. She ran back into the house and to Ian's bedside. As she kissed him, she whispered, "Oh Ian, I do love you, till death do us part, I'm sorry." She backed out of the room.

As she re-entered the car and buckled up, Shannon concentrated on Doctor Wallace's words, "He is doing fine. He is actually in good physical shape. He might just pull through this. Let's have faith and positive thoughts. Be patient Shannon. Watch him for any sign of movement."
She started the car, caressed the steering wheel and prayed, "God please help me!" She was still praying as she backed out of the driveway, "Please have mercy on me and Ian. Please let him awaken." That night she made an entry in her journal, "I hope Ian will be able to grow into a healthy old man, and will love me like that when I'm old."

June: Shannon loved to fish, and then to cook and share her catch. She spent many hours on the riverbank in front of her new home, doing just that. One such day, as she was sitting alone, trying to catch dinner, she heard the low roar of a boat in the distance. As it came closer, she realized it was Ruthie, Bill Reiner's mom.

As Ruthie stepped upon the pier, she apologized for not calling ahead. She asked if Shannon had a few minutes. Shannon assured her she did. Though she tried to sound casual, Ruthie seemed uncomfortable. Shannon hoped she had not somehow offended her new friend. After getting themselves a cold drink, the two women sat on the deck to talk. Shannon, never one to mince words, asked, "Ruthie, are you ok?"

Ruthie replied, "Yes." Then she added, "But Shannon, I've been 'wantin' to talk with you ever since you moved here." She continued, "Pat told me about your conversation about…you know."

Shannon, realizing Ruthie meant the strange occurrence at the bend of the road, asked her, "Did you ever think something was strange when you came up the road?"

Ruthie replied, "Yes, I always did, but, more than that, my twin sister, Renee', lives up in Queenstown. We grew up on the bay, and we both love the water. I moved here when I married my Woody. She married and moved up there. The last time I visited her, she told me I would have to come to Queenstown to visit her because she did not want to come down my way anymore. I was hurt. She said every that time she left my house; she suspected someone was chasing her. She was afraid. All those years and she never said a word to me. I never said anything about it either until Pat shared your conversation."

Ruthie paused, took a sip of her drink and said, "I am happy to be living back closer to the bay. Bill and Pat were afraid to tell me about the move. I was thrilled, but now I feel our happiness is at your expense."

Shannon asked, "What do you mean, at my expense?"

Ruthie, having a hard time discussing the possibility of a spirit living among them, finally blurted out, "Don't you see, if there is a ghost a 'hauntin' this area, you've inherited our ghost. Pat and I are at peace up there on the bay and you're stuck here with...you know."

Shannon smiled and said, "If that's what's bothering you, Ruthie, please relax. If Pat shared our conversation, then you must know I was aware of something unusual before I even bought the property. I'm here because I want to be, and I am very happy with my surroundings. I would be in paradise if only Ian was able to share this home." Her mind sadly wandered back to Ian's condition for a second, and then, regaining her composure, she added, "I will get to the bottom of the haunting, I just know it. It's probably why I was compelled to be here. Sounds like self-praise, but I do believe I was called here."

Shannon's obvious faith took Ruthie by surprise. She seemed very much at peace during the rest of their conversation.

When it was time for Ruthie's departure and she was stepping into her boat, she said, "Shannon, I am so glad you chose this place as your home."

Shannon thanked her, but inwardly, she was worried Ian might not think so. Watching Ruthie expertly prepare the boat for voyage, she thought about the stark difference in personalities of the two widowed sisters-in-law. Ruthie was outgoing and adventurous, not hesitating to go boating or driving alone, secure in her own abilities, while Martha was content to keep her neat home clean, work in her yard and make lunch for the two young farmers. She was very happy when her daughter, Sue and husband, Rob, purchased Bill and Pat's home. There she was, all snug and happy with her 'off-springs' living nearby, happy to just sit on the porch, enjoying her world.

Ruthie once told Shannon, that even when they were young, Martha was a super homebody. Their deceased husbands, who were twins, were also homebodies. Ruthie seemed to be the only adventurous soul in the quartet.

Watching Ruthie's boat disappear around the bend, and gazing at its remaining wake, Shannon smiled at the very agile boats-woman. She wondered if Ian would be angry if she bought a boat.

Sitting by the water relaxed Shannon some days and angered her on others. She often wondered, "How many lives were lived on this very spot? How many lives lost, how many feet walked where I now walk?" Whatever her mood, she, as did Sean and Kaitlin Rose, began and ended each day sitting by, or looking at the river. It usually provided a calming effect. It did that afternoon, for a while. That joy was short lived.

She started walking toward the house, but stopped abruptly and looked over the field, to the big rock. Something compelled her to walk through the field toward it. As she approached it, an extreme sadness filled her heart. It was as if she were sobbing deep within her soul. She kept repeating, "What is wrong? What is wrong?" No tears arose in her, but she wanted to cry aloud.

She stood there for a moment. Finally, she whispered, "I wonder how many babies were rocked to sleep here by this rock, by this wonderful river. How many dances danced and songs sung." She felt as if she were remembering rather than imagining. Laying her hand on the stone's rough surface, she caressed it, as a person would do while reassuring another person. She smiled rather sadly, and then turned, and began her walk home.

Suddenly, out of the corner of her eye, she caught a glimpse of a young woman standing nearby. Almost breathless, she stood very still. So did the young woman. Suddenly, the young woman turned, and ran behind the rock. Shannon was shaking so violently, that she almost fell. On previous visits to the area, she was startled and frightened, but compelled to visit the rock. That day was different. She felt threatened. She spirit was becoming more desperate and aggressive.

Without looking to see if anyone was behind her, Shannon ran through the field as fast as she could toward home.

CHAPTER THIRTEEN
Summer on the Choptank

July, August and September: came and went so quickly. Several family members and friends came to visit throughout the summer. Shannon was always so glad to see all of them, and sad to see them leave, as if her other life, the link to the old Ian, was leaving with them, but the couple sharing her home comforted her. They all worked like balls of fire all summer.

With the help of Chester and Michael, Sean renovated the studio and turned it into an adorable little two-room cottage. Chester had previously installed plumbing, so establishing waterworks was easy. He said he needed his own tinkle area when he was working. That brought laughter from Sean and Michael, and a blush to the cheeks of Kaitlin Rose. Pat called the new cottage "An adorable work of art."

On weekends, Sean and Michael worked like a team. Shannon was beginning to feel as if they were working for her comfort as a widow. For seven months in their new home, Ian gave no sign of awakening.

When Chester Fargo turned eighty years old, he had given up driving, so Ruthie would call ahead, and then drop him off to work with Sean. He loved tinkering around the place. It gave him great comfort, as if he had never sold it, but was just sharing it with friends.

Sean appreciated Chester's help, but worried about the older man over-working. Shannon said not to worry, if the old man died working on the home his love built, it would be his heaven. That fact gave Sean little comfort, but still they worked on. Pat was afraid Chester was offending Shannon by helping Sean. It did not. No one knew the extent of understanding shared by Shannon and Chester. Shannon was growing to love the place as gently as he did.

Chester genuinely cared about Ian. He was so gentle with

him, when, from time to time, he would offer to sit with him, if everyone else wanted to work outside together. He seemed to love Ian like a son. Kaitlin Rose had remarked, "Like a little boy."

Chester's own son, Pat's uncle, died at the age of eighteen. Pat shared some of the details with Shannon, one Sunday, as they were leaving church:

"It happened just before my mom left for school in Baltimore, even before my parents were married."

Pat continued, "So my grandparents basically lost both of their children about the same time. Of course, my mother and grandfather do visit pretty often."

Shannon had asked, "So you grew up in Baltimore, right?"

Pat answered, "Yes, my parents still live there. My mother said she hated this place. I didn't understand why. When we came to visit, I always wanted to stay. Often, I did stay here all summer with my grandparents, actually against my mom's wishes. She said the place always gave her the creeps. She thought it was haunte…"

Instead of finishing her sentence, Pat looked directly into Shannon's eyes and asked, "Shannon, I hate to ask you this, here, on the church property, but are we, as Christians, supposed to believe in spirits? Do you still really think it is…you know? I keep thinking about it. I mean, I hated to walk up the road. I was scared. Bill always teased me about it."

Shannon nodded, "You have to believe what truly happens to you. No one can tell you to believe, or not to believe. That spirit is among us, for whatever reason, I don't know why. It's a fact. What can we do, but believe? It does not take away my faith in my Creator. How about you?" Pat smiled and nodded in agreement and took her leave to re-join her family.

After the conversation with Pat on Sunday, Shannon began feeling bad about the promise she had made to the 'Spirit' the day she and Kim were walking up the road. It was a promise she would be back and everything would, 'be all right.'

She thought to herself, "Good grief, now I'm feeling bad about a broken promise I made to a 'GHOST'. I must really be losing it." She had been so preoccupied that she had almost forgotten her promise and simply dealt with the sad feeling every time she walked up the road. Suddenly, she exclaimed, **"Up the road!"**

She realized every time she had the strange feeling, she was walking, or driving, up the road. She wondered, "Why not when I walk down the road? Why hasn't Kaitlin Rose ever mentioned it?" The vision of a young girl's sad face, memories of her running alongside the car, of touching the huge cold rock by the river, of literally seeing her by the rock, all arose in her memory, haunting her as she drove home.

The next day, while they were canning some of Sean's harvest, Shannon decided to question Kaitlin Rose about it. She asked, "Kaitlin Rose, are you ok living here?"

The startled, gentle, Irish woman, near tears, was hurt. She almost whimpered, "Aren't you pleased with me, Shannon?"

Shannon answered, "Oh, yes. Yes I am! Please don't think I'm not. I would be so lost without you and Sean. I just mean is there anything about the location that upsets you. Like, do you ever feel….?"

Kaitlin Rose interrupted Shannon's question, "Like the place is haunted, Shannon?"

Shannon almost dropped a pot full of canning jars. She was surprised when Kaitlin Rose, in a very casual manner, answered, "Well, yes. I'm sure 'tis haunted. I pray for the poor thing every night. God rest her wee soul. She came to a sad end, for sure. A sadness comes over me every time I walk back home from Sue's or Evelyn's house. I always feel like the young lady is pleading to me."

Shannon thought, "Back home from Sues, hmm, **up the**

road! Not down the road." She asked Kaitlin Rose, "Does Sean believe in the haunting?"

Kaitlin Rose answered, "Oh sure, I confided in him the very week we were waiting for you to arrive.

The three of us, Michael, Sean and m'self, had taken a wee walk to investigate the neighborhood. I felt it as we were returning to your cottage, and I have felt it every time since. Neither Sean nor Michael seemed to notice anything out of the ordinary. Sean has never noticed any feeling whatsoever since, but he knows me, and he knows if I say it's haunted, it's haunted for sure."

Shannon asked Kaitlin Rose if she ever noticed the feeling when she was walking, or driving down the road. Kaitlin Rose said she did not. Whether it helped her detecting or not, Shannon had a general idea as to where the spirit lingered. What she was going to do with that information was another matter.

CHAPTER FOURTEEN
If Martha Doesn't Know it, Then...

October: The month in which Shannon and Ian were married, and the anniversary of the month which concluded their last month-long vacation.

Shannon awoke on October 1. Ian did not. Everything seemed so matter of fact. Just get the work done, tend to Ian, eat and go to bed. She looked over to check on him. Kaitlin Rose was already tending him. Shannon thought, "She's so good with him."

Shannon arose, said "Good Morning," and quietly left the room. She walked toward the back door, saying to Sean, "You guys go ahead and eat without me. I'll eat later. I'm going for a long walk." Sean nodded.

She trembled as she walked down the road, remembering the young girl, and then she thought of Ian. She looked toward the rock, and at the beautiful scenery. There awoke in her an overwhelming depression. She thought, "This place could be such a haven if only..." She wanted to scream aloud. Instead, she gave herself the old familiar pep talk, "I've got to get a grip on myself. I'm no good to anyone, especially myself, this way."

Every time she felt this unsettling sorrow, she was afraid it was a sign Ian was dying. She had no clue as to what the young girl's role in the total situation was, except she was definitely a distracting haunting presence, and was wearing heavily on Shannon's challenging spirit. Fighting her feelings, she briskly continued her walk. She crossed the field, walked back past the house and continued walking down the road. She did not realize she had gone so far, until she heard Martha's familiar voice,

"Good morning, Sweet Irish."

Bill's Aunt Martha was sitting on her front porch, enjoying the morning sun. Sweet Irish was the name she gave to both Shannon and Kaitlin Rose.

Shannon usually just waved and walked on. Martha loved company and it was usually hard to get away, once you got into conversation, but that day was different. Shannon was glad for a break in her down trodden walk. She greeted her new friend. As she stepped up upon the porch, she asked, "Martha, do you have a couple of minutes?"

Martha replied, "Sure, I've got nothing, but time." She got them both a cup of coffee.

They spent a few minutes in simple tête-à-tête. Then, to approach the subject of the haunting, Shannon jumped right in with her questioning, "Martha, have you always lived in this area?"

"Yep." was Martha's reply, "I'm told my ancestors owned all of this land." Shannon smiled at the sound of Martha's 'Old World' Eastern Shore colloquial speech.

Shannon had heard about Martha's ancestry and wanted to talk to her about it. She asked, "Do you know much about your ancestors?"

Martha began relating what little she knew of her ancestry,

"Seems my folk were early Americans, First Americans, actually. Like I said and 'M' owned all this land. 'Th's' tales my up-line grandmother was of the Choptank Tribe. Some folk say a soldier captured her, but she killed him and escaped.

"Years later, folk told the story that the truth was he actually loved her, and they ran away so's they could live as married folk. There's tales they had eight kids, they did! For several years, the family scattered and lived just about everywhere. Later, one of the descendants, my great-great-grandfather, knowing of his First American heritage, and that all this land once belonged to his people, decided to return to this area, and take legal claim of what should have been his people's land, by ownership of birth. He did return as a very wealthy man. He bought up as much land as he could in his lifetime, so his descendants would

own the land of their ancestors."

Martha added, "That's about all I know. I'm just glad he came back here. I guess I'm guilty as the next person, about not learning much about my kin. However, there's some real good books over at the library about the folks who settled this area, and the ancients who lived here hundreds of years ago."

After Martha regaled Shannon with several lengthy stories, Shannon spoke softly to her, "Martha, some people say this area is haunted. What do you think?"

Martha answered, "M's folks who think so, maybe t's so, maybe not. I just pay no never mind. If it is, or not or ever was, no one has ever been hurt for the haunting. There's been tales for generations, of some woman dying over there near the big rock a long time ago and she haunts the place. There's always stories been told 'bout it, but I personally think somebody just made up the story one Halloween night."

Martha's mind seemed to wander, "We used to have lots of picnics there in Chester's field and no harm ever come to anyone. It was a lot of fun in those days."

Shannon asked, "Why did you stop having them."

Martha replied, "Can't say for sure. Think it had to do with Chester's son being killed, I reckon. That's about the time we quit having them."

After seeming to drift off for a moment, Martha continued,

"He was their first born, had just graduated from high school and was on a fun trip to Baltimore with two other graduates. An intoxicated driver drove thru a red light and hit them as they crossed Fayette Street. The other two boys survived. A sad day, I can tell you. We stopped having the picnics in Chester's field after that." Martha's mind wandered back to the accident, "He was such a good boy, pity! His parents were so depressed. Then, later their daughter, Marie, Pat's mama, graduated from high school and went to some special school in Baltimore. She

121

never came back, except to visit. Even then, she never stays long. They were sure sad folk, Chester and Arlene. Thank God for Patricia's return. She sure made her grandparents very happy the day she married my nephew."

Martha repeated, "Those picnics just never got started up again. Such a pity. Sure was fun in those days with Chester and Arlene and everybody dancing on the floor that Chester always built." She repeated, "Sure was fun in those days. Many things changed that summer. Lots of things." The two women visited for more than two hours. This pleased Martha.

On her way home, Shannon thought about the name Martha gave the field near the big rock, 'Chester's Field'. It sounded so nice and homey. For the moment, she was at peace. Even with knowing what she would encounter as she walked up the road, she was ok. She also felt Kaitlin Rose's theory about a young girl was right on target. It could be a young First American girl, but she wondered why she was haunting so aggressively.

As she walked up the road, Shannon thought to herself, "Wonder why Aunt Martha never experienced the feeling, or ever spoke of it?" She thought, "Maybe, just maybe, Martha's ancestry, no matter how faint the knowledge, kept her from having any fear of spirits, or, perhaps she feels it would be yoking with evil spirits if she even remotely acknowledged any super natural being near her." Chuckling, she even imagined a scenario where only non-First American women were being haunted and Martha was not, because she 'belonged.'

As Shannon walked, she continued her theory, "Maybe Martha does feel something and hates to admit it. So, what does it matter? Stop rambling, Shannon Fitzpatrick. Who cares about what she thinks or feels? Not me. Oh heck, whatever!" She continued her walk, feeling the same love for the river that people had shared for many generations.

Reaching the bend in the road, a sudden feeling of sadness interrupted her random thoughts. She could have been walking blindfolded and known exactly where she was. As usual, she looked beyond the field, to the huge rock and the river. The river was always her source of solace.

She felt as if someone was watching her. For a few minutes, she even allowed her imagination to create a figure to go along with her feeling. She abruptly ceased walking. Then, deciding to go to the river, she began a leaf-crushing walk through the field. She stopped at the rock and touched the cold stone with her right hand. Surprisingly, for the moment, she did not have any fear or feel any sadness. She simply said, "Don't be afraid."

Realizing the absurdity of her statement, she thought, "I should be the one afraid." Thinking her imagination was controlling her sanity and creating an imaginary creature, she turned, swat her hand in the air, as if to dismiss her thoughts, and began her walk back to the road.

A sudden breeze arose and just as suddenly, something seemed to touch her arm. She whirled around, and for a moment, she was looking through a cloud. There seemed to be a face. She felt as if she were looking into sad eyes. She stared, seemingly frozen. Then, she was surely afraid. Severely shaken, she ran as fast as she could through the field, to the safety of her home.

Shannon knew she dared not relate the story to the cousins. They were already concerned for her mental health. The entire 'Ian Experience' was draining on everyone's energy. The 'Wait and See' plan was becoming more difficult.

Using the excuse that she wanted to sit alone and read, Shannon retreated to her small room at the back of the house for the rest of the day, leaving the care of Ian totally to Kaitlin Rose. Alone in her room, she nervously recalled the recent incident. She wondered if the stress of losing Ian to his immobility was playing havoc with her mental health, causing her to create an imaginative, sad woman to share her grief. She wept. Mentally exhausted, she fell asleep clinging to one of Ian's shirts, rolled into a pillow. She slept through the night.

Very early the next morning, realizing that she had left Ian alone, Shannon ran to the bedroom. Kaitlin Rose was sleeping in the lounger. She had spent the night with Ian, allowing Shannon to sleep.

After breakfast, Shannon went out to run errands. Remembering Martha saying the library had 'some good books', she decided, if she ever solved any mystery, it might begin there. She borrowed a stack of books dealing with the history of the area and some of folklore. As she was scanning through them, trying to select the one to read first, her mind nervously recalled the previous day. By that time, she convinced herself that her stress produced an imaginary episode. She half-chuckled, "With my imagination, I could write one of these. Gotta get a grip."

Later, she showed the books to Kaitlin Rose, and shared the conversation she had with Martha the previous day. Leaving out the incident by the river's edge, and skirting around her experience, she asked, "If there really is something going on in this area, is it up to me to solve any of its mystery? No one else has ever thought of doing it. Why should I even worry about it? What does it matter? Martha said no one had ever been hurt for the haunting." (There, she used the word, 'haunting.') "Why can't it just go on as it is? It's obviously been a part of the history of this area for a long time!"

Kaitlin Rose answered, "I think it's time to help the poor creature." Then she asked, "Do you think maybe you were called to come here, Shannon? Maybe your spirit connected with her and you are her salvation."

Kaitlin Rose always referred to the presence as, the 'Wee One' or 'Poor Little Thing' or 'Sad Little Girl'. She seemed to have strong intuitive abilities. They looked over the books for a while, and then went about their own routines.

Later in the day, looking over the stack of books, Shannon remembered the night of the book signing. She had purchased two books. On the front of one of them, was a First Native American woman running and looking up to the sky. It reminded her of the trauma of that night. She decided the

Maryland History from the bookstore would be the first one to read. Convinced that she would find some connection to the haunting, she read all day and again the next, barely ate or slept. She always found fascination in history, and did enjoy the history and cultures of the area she now called home. If it were not for one of the cousins bringing an occasional snack, she probably would have gone without eating.

Through the small collection of books, she gathered very little pertinent information, not enough to be of any 'help' (per Kaitlin Rose's urging). Actually, she was not very sure she wanted to 'help' any unproven creature. She decided she had wasted her time and would just concentrate on getting through her anniversary month.

Taking care of Ian, and doing lots of canning and freezing kept Shannon busy. Conversations with Sean and Kaitlin Rose, as they worked together, and the occasional visits from Chester and Michael, were her salvation. She seemed to be passing on helping the wee creature. Kaitlin Rose was not worried though. She knew the desire to solve the mystery would surface again in Shannon. She had grown to know her new cousin. She knew her unsettling nature, when faced with a challenge. She felt Shannon just needed time.

Shannon had grown to love the Choptank River area. Nevertheless, one day, October 22, she almost wished she had never moved there. She wondered why she was even there. She was restless. Her wedding anniversary with Ian was only a day away. She felt slightly more connected to the area after reading the borrowed book, but uneasy, as if something was stirring inside of her. After dreaming several nights in a row about the face on one of the books, and awakening to the memory of her experience by the rock, she could not shake the strange uneasy feeling that waxed and waned in her soul.

That night, a very vivid dream awakened her. She quickly looked over at Ian to be sure he was breathing. He was sleeping. She sighed, "Just sleeping. Maybe the dreams are a good sign though, Ian. Tomorrow is our anniversary. I hope my dream is a good sign." She looked over at him. Then, quickly and silently, reprimanded herself, "Stop it Shannon Fitzpatrick, there are no signs, no good signs, no happy signs, just fading hope. Nothing!"

The same old fear was rising in her spirit. Nevertheless, she kissed him, and whispered gently, "Good morning, Darling. Please let this be the day you awaken. I love you." The only response, the sound of machines, sent a chill up her spine. She dressed and began thinking about their anniversary. She wanted to cry, but would not in front of Ian, afraid he might hear her in his sleep state.

Putting on hand lotion, she wrung her hands until they hurt. Looking at her hands, Shannon thought about a poem Ian wrote about them, how he loved to hold them. Now, they were simply hands spent caring for him and his machines, and working, working, working.

Ignoring breakfast, she by-passed the kitchen, and exited by the back door. Instead of starting her walk by the river, she headed for the road, crying as she walked, "I can't take this anymore. I just can't."

The sun was almost visible. Shannon usually loved to walk and watch its arrival. That day, she ran until she reached the bend in the road. She turned, looked toward the river, to the rock in front of it, and then to the sky. She cried out to the river, "Why am I even here? I thought I would love you. I thought you would help me with Ian. I thought you would bring magic to my life and peace to my soul. You are no help! You are a burden to me! You and your ghosts! Just swallow them up keep them to yourself and leave me alone!"

To whom was she speaking? She did not know. She just knew in her soul, for all the time she had lived there, she was not alone when she walked on her own property.

In the beginning, the illusion was a challenge to Shannon. She actually welcomed it, because she was a problem solver. She thought it might give her satisfaction to solve its mystery. She had felt, with some investigation, she would find the source of the entity haunting the area. Woman Folk rumored about a haunting woman for generations. However, none of the local history books supported the theory. Most people did not even believe a problem ever existed. Apparently, only a few women spoke of it and most folk dismissed the stories as simple ghost stories.

Shannon continued to lament, "Who was I kidding? There is no spirit! You don't exist!" Then realizing how irrational she sounded, she asked, "Am I going crazy? Who are you, here in this place?" Chastising herself, she said, "What am I thinking? What am I thinking? Am I losing my mind?"

Because of her anguish, Shannon's mind was darting from thought to thought. She inwardly cried as she ran, "There's no spirit, except the spirit of my own fears. Stop it Shannon Fitzpatrick! Stop thinking! Stop talking to Ghosts!" She kept running until she reached the bus stop, crying aloud by this time, trying to look as if she were not when a car passed by.

Beaten, she started the walk home. She needed to be near Ian. Feeling bad about the outburst, she stopped and prayed, "Forgive me Father. Forgive my sins. Please help me to understand." All of her religious teachings, which she still believed and practiced, taught her about one Holy Spirit, but a small, still voice inside of her told her that one of God's children, even if it were dead to our world, was in trouble. She finally believed that its spirit cried out to passers-by for help, particularly to women.

Shannon did love Ian very much. However, that day, she almost hated him for leaving her. She remembered that he had said, "We'll have a late dinner. I've got some great news." For months, she had tried, unsuccessfully, to remember his exact words.

She wondered, "Could he have found the perfect property to show me?"

What was Ian's great news?

Perhaps she would never know. No one had ever contacted her about any property he may have considered, nor did she find any paperwork concerning any properties he may have seen. She wondered if he would remember anything if, or when, he did awaken. Would she ever find out what Ian's last thoughts were?

Last thoughts! Those words caused Shannon to think that she may have been responsible for his accident by urging him to hurry to the bookstore. She looked ahead to the bend in the road. She stopped. Knowing what was coming, she stood very still, repeating, "Who is she? Who is she?"

As she approached the area, the same sad feeling came over her. Logically, she knew it was not tangible, but she and the other women who experienced it believed it was real. They all had the same feeling of sadness. Some of them, like her, because of their religious faith, felt guilt at acknowledging such things.

That day, her guilt turned to anger. She cried sarcastically, "I can't deal with your sadness today. I have my own." She was in no mood to help anyone, especially someone or something she could not really see or touch, or even prove its existence.

Realizing the situation she was in, and the irrationality of her thoughts, Shannon lamented, "Damn you Ian! Damn you!" Instantly regretting the terrible curse, she prayed aloud, "Oh God, what am I saying? Oh Ian, Forgive me! Please God, Forgive me! Forgive me! Forgive me!" As if she were in sudden shock, running away from her own self, she bolted through the field toward the river, the sound of crushing leaves her only sign she was actually moving. When she reached the big rock, she collapsed at its base. Tears, usually only allowed to surface briefly, and then shoved deep within her belly, flowed freely from her exhausted body. She lay on the ground, weeping. Her face was dirty from sand and soil. She wanted to bury her pain deeper and deeper, to escape her anguish. She wept until she was weak, slowly arose, and then walked to the river.

Standing at water's edge, Shannon had the feeling of falling in. She almost wanted to. She was frightfully aware of someone standing beside her. She felt a slight tug on her arm, but saw no one. She looked down. There was an opaque vision of an arm. She knew for certain, the vision she had been seeing was the spirit of a young girl. It appeared to be an ancient. That morning, she was not sure if the girl needed help, or wanted to help. She made a gesture of friendship, by crossing her arms over her own chest. The image disappeared.

Shannon's mind was racing with uncertainty, compassion and fear. She cried to the spirit, "Come back. Please come back." She felt the mist from the river. The ghostly apparition frightened her. However, she knew the answer to her own peace was reliant on her dealing with, and solving the reason for the young girl's apparent sadness. What was she to do? She had no control. Exhausted by her experience, she knelt, dipped her hands in the water, splashed her face and started another slow walk home.

Kaitlin Rose watched Shannon from the kitchen window. She was aware that Sean, who also watched Shannon from a distance those days, was prepared to perform a rescue. Relieved when Shannon began to walk home, Sean went in for breakfast. As Shannon came through the door, Kaitlin Rose asked, "Are you ok, Luv?"

Shannon's only reply was "I'm ok." Sean gave Kaitlin Rose a 'Leave her alone' look. Kaitlin Rose silently agreed. Sean asked, "Ready for some coffee, Luv?"

Shannon nodded. Realizing they could certainly tell she had been crying, Shannon felt she owed them an explanation. She simply stated, "Today is mine and Ian's anniversary." That was enough.

On Friday afternoon, Michael arrived. It was also his birthday week. Shannon hoped a miracle would happen; that Ian would awaken during those special days. It happened like that all the time in the old movies. However, the weekend went as usual, quiet, but nice.

On Saturday, Kaitlin Rose made a special Irish dinner for Michael's birthday celebration. On Sunday, when he was leaving, Shannon walked him to the car. Every time he left her, she felt her only real link with Ian was also leaving. However, as she walked into the house, she saw two wonderful people, who were not only related to Ian, but genuinely cared for her as well. She realized she did have a very wonderful family bond. Very early the next day, she awoke as if someone was calling to her. "Yes." she answered. She looked over to Ian's bed, anticipating her miracle. He was in his usual peaceful sleep state.

The machines were doing what they were supposed to do, keeping Ian alive. It was dawn. She quietly went out for her morning walk. She looked to the river and meekly smiled at the thought that the rock really did look like a giant bird or angel wing. She walked past the field, to the Pendry's Farm, and then past Martha's house. She stopped to rest in little covered shed Bill's father built for the school bus children, took a drink of water from her water bottle, put the bottle back in the pouch and began her walk home.

CHAPTER FIFTEEN
Face to Face

The road curved to the right. Shannon accelerated her pace, and kept it strong until she reached the area near the big rock, determined to ignore any feelings that might arise. However, something compelled her to turn and run into the field. She obeyed her instincts, crushing the autumn leaves as she ran. Breathlessly, she reached the rock. She knelt and, as she did every time she went to the area, touched the rock and prayed more fervently than she had ever prayed before. She felt as if someone was praying with her, maybe for her. It was as if another hand was caressing hers. She clung to the rock, as if to embrace it, as if it had the power to heal her broken heart. She lay her face against the cold stone and sobbed.

Ignoring the roughness, she violently rubbed the boulder. Her hands and face were becoming bloody and salty from her tears. Leaning against the rock, she slid down to the ground, and lay there face down in the sand. Random thoughts and feelings waxed and waned in her mind. She felt she could just stay there and await death. Her anguish was that great.

She slowly closed her eyes. Something compelled her to open them. Through the morning mist, she thought she saw a beautiful young girl standing by the river. The young girl seemed to be holding out her hands. Shannon had no fear. Strangely, she felt love. She arose, walked over to the clouded apparition, and tried to take hold of a hand, but felt only the cool morning mist. The vision disappeared, but the love remained.

She looked up to the autumn sky, raised her arms as if in awe of the beautiful sky and prayed, "Please Father God, forgive me. Forgive me for failing my love, causing him shame in your sight. Forgive me for hurting my loved ones. Please take away the shame of my sins. Let the sun feel warm on my face. Let the moon be a light for my broken soul. Bless all my

131

people, and do not grieve them for my sin. Help me fight the evil spirit. Father Spirit, Please hear me! Please hear me! Please hear me! Let me come to you in the clouds as a good spirit. Let my face be, again, clean in your sight."

The realization of what she was praying overwhelmed Shannon. The words she uttered were startling, unfamiliar and frightening. She stood motionless, arms outstretched, staring out over the river, almost afraid to breathe. A very gentle breeze seemed to be passing through her, causing her to catch her breath and loose her balance. She struggled to stand firm. Someone else seemed to be speaking for her, for she nervously cried out, "Annasqua, Annasqua."

Shannon inhaled deeply, realizing that she was no longer depressed or afraid. Though she was exhausted, she felt embraced by a serene love. She looked back at the rock. Something was different. She was not sure what it was. However, for the first time since she had been coming to that area, she felt gentle. Somehow, she knew her 'friend' was gone. It was ok. She cupped her hands, gathered some water, and washed her bloody, stinging face. Her body was weak, but she walked back to the giant rock and lingered long enough to caress it.

She began a homeward walk through the field. Midway, she turned and looked back. She smiled gently, knowing that the previous haunting experiences were not of danger. They were, rather, of a pleading spirit and a hurting heart.

She looked up, closed her eyes and said a quiet thankful prayer; feeling hopeful that she had, in some way, helped that hurting heart find relief from its grief, and that God understood her believing in spirits, she continued her walk. Arriving at home, she said nothing about it to the cousins, but they recognized the look of contentment. They also noticed her wounds, but said nothing about them. She took a shower, tended to her wounds and relaxed on the sofa in the den. Recalling the incident, she could not fully understand what she had said by the river, nor why she spoke so strangely. She was sure, the word "Annasqua" was a name, but wondered why she cried to it, or for it. She reasoned it was probably all the folklore in the books she had been reading. She closed her eyes and actually smiled. She slept late in the day, got up, checked on Ian, ate and wrote in her journal.

It was a lovely October evening, not the perfect anniversary, but serenity was her gift. She reasoned that Ian was still alive, so there was still hope. She relaxed on her bed, and listened to his 'saved' voice on her cell phone messaging. Although his voice made her sad, she felt ok. She caressed his shoulder and said, "You'll awaken soon. I know it." For the first time in a long while, she actually felt positive. She closed her tired eyes and went to sleep.

October had been a busy month so it seemed to pass quickly. Sean harvested his crops, while Shannon and Kaitlin Rose canned or froze the bounty. Shannon spent her evenings filling the journal with the events of the day. As she had done almost every night since Ian's accident, she read those pages to him, in hopes he heard her. If he did not understand her words, possibly the sound of her voice penetrated his brain waves.

Jennifer, Andrew Marshal's widow, planned to spend Thanksgiving week with her children, so she visited the Fitzpatrick's new home in late October. She brought Shannon up to date with the 'happenings' at the theater. Her face showed the pain of losing Andrew. It was obvious she needed a get-away. The three women spent much of her visit in the kitchen, canning and freezing vegetables and fruit. Shannon apologized that she had to keep working, but Jennifer was thrilled to be doing 'country' stuff. A lot of laughter came from the kitchen during the week. Sean worked inside, and kept watch on Ian. Jennifer was very impressed with the smoothness of their duties.

When it was time to depart, Shannon walked Jennifer to the car. Jennifer said, "You are a great team. Ian is lucky to have you guys. He will awaken soon and tell you himself." She looked upward, "Be sure to remember 'He' knows and cares! You and Ian will be ok very soon." Shannon nodded.

November happened so quickly. Suddenly, there it was, Thanksgiving. Kim, Keith and Michael came for the weekend. They had as wonderful a Thanksgiving as they could. Sean and Kaitlin Rose took Kim and Keith to services on the eve. Michael and Shannon spent the evening sitting by Ian's bed and talking to him.

Their next day, their Thanksgiving dinner was very 'country'. Sean proudly served his crops. There was a lovely fire burning in the stone fireplace that Chester built with his bare hands (as he loved to tell folk). As she toasted her family and friends before dinner Shannon said, "I don't know what I would have done without all of you." Michael said a proper Irish blessing for the American holiday. The day was wonderful, except Ian was not sitting with them at the table.

The group spent the day after Thanksgiving decorating for Christmas. When the weekend was over and the visitors were gone, Shannon spent a restless night in her twin bed beside Ian, aching to hold him and have him hold her. She cried herself to sleep. The three cousins spent the rest of November preparing for the winter. Previously, Chester had warned Sean and Michael to make sure they stored plenty of firewood. His exact words were:

"You just never know when that might be the only heat you'll have. Maybe you should have a generator, just in case you lose electricity."

Michael panicked when he heard that. He purchased a generator with plenty of gas tanks. He said, "No use tempting fate." Shannon wanted to protest, but resisted, for she knew Ian's life support machines needed electricity. She decided to take the help Michael wanted to give.

CHAPTER SIXTEEN
Waiting for a Christmas Miracle

December: Sean cut down a Christmas tree, and planted a baby one. The trio tried to embrace the true meaning of Christmas. They worked out a schedule for church and Christmas shopping, made homemade ornaments and baked cookies.

Shannon was not enthusiastic about Christmas shopping, but wanted to buy gifts for her family and friends. As she was walking through the stores, looking at the Christmas decorations and hearing Christmas music and chatter of shoppers, she remembered wonderful Christmas Holidays spent with her parents and then, later, with Ian and his parents.

Thinking ahead to the holidays, she felt almost obligated to invite Chester and his family over to see her beautifully decorated home. She was not really in the spirit of giving or entertaining, but determined to keep a semblance of Christmas spirit. As she was purchasing a sweater for Sean. She spied a gorgeous leather jacket, which looked as if it absolutely belonged on Ian's back. She caressed it lightly. Feeling the soft leather under her palm caused her to feel shaky. She quickly paid for her items, left the store and drove home.

Opening the garage door with the remote was truly automatic, for Shannon hardly remembered doing so. Realizing this, she turned off the engine and sat in the car for a few minutes. She rested her head on the steering wheel, trying to get her emotions under control before going inside. It was not working.

She got out of the car. Instead of going into the house, she walked to the riverside. She stood looking at the river for a long time. The picture in front of her was magnificent. Light snow was covering the ground. Chunks of ice were floating in sections of the river. Gulls were flying overhead. Ducks were sitting in formation on the riverbank. The water's edge was churning from the rushing wind of winter's toll. The rocks seemed to be groaning from the impact of the 'wild winter' water.

An excited, scared feeling arose in Shannon. Being so used to those feelings, she just sighed and walked back around to the garage, gathered her bundles from the car, and walked into the house.

As she stepped in the kitchen, she heard Kaitlin Rose screaming for Sean. She ran down the hallway toward the bedroom, yelling, "What's wrong?"

Kaitlin Rose was almost in tears as she cried out, "I thought he moved, but then it was as if he stopped breathing for a minute!" Sean called 911, and then started the car. As soon as the medical personnel secured Ian in the ambulance, they all left for the hospital. Doctor Wallace was waiting for them. As they hurriedly walked alongside the stretcher holding Ian's motionless body, Shannon nervously asked, "What do you think, Doctor Wallace?" Almost begging for an answer, she repeated, "What's wrong?"

Doctor Wallace answered, "Shannon, let's just be calm, could be nothing, maybe just spasms, he's had them before." Realizing her anxious confusion, he quickly added, "Or it could be our miracle. Let's wait and see, ok?"

Shannon nervously stated, "Kaitlin Rose said it was not a spasm. It was movement. She was sure of it." She wanted to believe Kaitlin Rose, and asked the doctor, "Why did it look like he almost stopped breathing? Why did the machine not breathe for him?"

Doctor Wallace continued to be reassuring. He said, "Don't know. We will find out. We'll give him, and his machinery, a complete work up." He continued walking alongside the stretcher carrying Ian. Shannon went to the waiting room with the cousins, muttering a meek, "Ok." She called Michael. Settling down to wait, she wondered if she was witnessing her husband's final days, and if his movements were merely a flicker of light before he drew his final breath.

Michael came to the hospital as soon as Shannon called.

He stayed as long as he could, only to go back home with a heavy heart. He promised to finish his year-end business, and be back in a few days. Because of the holiday break, he was able to stay for at least two weeks.

Christmas, Hanukah, Kwanzaa, the season of giving, of the scent of wood burning fireplaces, and the awesome feeling of new birth, had arrived. Shannon and Michael were still waiting for their miracle on Christmas morning. There was none.

Shannon's heart was actually becoming hardened at the thought of miracles. She had begun to concentrate on Ian's maintenance more than thinking of him as her husband. The sad issue was that she was beginning to question the God she had worshipped, and leaned on, all of her life. Realizing this thought sickened her. She felt remorse for those thoughts and prayed often about it.

Once again, Michael, Shannon and Ian were spending a Christmas and New Year Holiday in a hospital.

After the holidays, Michael came every weekend. The cousins promised the decorations would stay intact until Ian came home. Shannon was trying hard to keep the faith that she would be taking him home, awake. She went home only occasionally. Doctor Wallace wanted to keep Ian in the hospital for a few more days. Shannon hoped he saw something she did not. She saw no change.

January: The days had all become one. The hospital staff accepted Shannon staying in Ian's room. Actually, she was a big help. Doctor Wallace was attentive, but Shannon was beginning to feel he was giving up hope of Ian ever awakening. Sensing her uncertainty, he made every effort to appear positive.

Shannon often slept in the big overstuffed chair in Ian's room. The staff, accustomed to her being there, and to her late night, mid-morning departures, never bothered to awaken her. Early one morning, she awoke from an 'almost' sleep state. She looked over at Ian and her heart started to pound. She was tired to the point of exhaustion. She cried inwardly, "It may be like this forever. I might as well ask Doctor Wallace to release him to a long-term care facility. I suppose I should start making arrangements. I'm not doing him any good. Maybe I've actually hindered his progress by trying to take care of him at home."

She felt beaten. The one glimmer of hope she had back in December was a sad reminder of that fact. She thought, "Twenty-seven months! Twenty-seven months. He is never going to awaken. It's over. I've got to admit it." She sobbed as she walked out of the room. There was no reason to sit and stare at him. Nothing ever changed. Having made the Care Facility decision and feeling as if she had just lost a long, hard battle, she needed to rest. She left the hospital, and went home to relate her decision to the cousins.

The fence, the gate and the river looked like a beautiful picture on a Christmas card. With the fields totally mowed, the house was in view from the road. Shannon mocked, "Sure! The perfect home is what folks driving by might think." She angrily told the morning sky, "Well it sure isn't perfect." She started to step upon the deck, but, instead, she walked to the small dock by the river.

Getting angrier, she grumbled, "What was I thinking? I gave up a perfectly good career, a home with very little work involved, all my friends, and spent most of our money. For what?" She repeated aloud, "For what?"

Instead of returning to the house, she decided to walk down the road. When she passed the field accommodating the big rock, she looked to the water and let out a long sigh. Unlike previous times when she yelled hysterically at the river, she simply looked up to the sky and meekly lamented, "I don't even know you. Why am I here? It was all about you and your ghosts. It was never about me! You needed me. I did not need you. I needed Ian."

Realizing she was turning her anger toward the God she had served all of her life, Shannon felt ashamed. Still, feeling abandoned by the same God, her voice became more angry and her cries louder, "God, don't you know me? Do you not hear me? Don't you love me? I'm here! Can't you see me? I've done all the right things all my life. Now I need you! You just don't care. You just do not care! I honored and obeyed my parents. I've read your word. I even lived by your word most of the time. Still you do not hear me."

Raising her arms to the sky, Shannon lamented, "Where are you God? Where are you? I did what Kally asked of me. I finished high school even after she died. I went to college. I took that as divine providence, that you sent me to find my Ian. I thought that was what you wanted for me. I was wrong. You've taken everything away from me. Now I'm here where I don't belong and still, you forsake me. Don't you even care? Don't you even love me anymore? Did you ever care? Did you ever?" Her words of anger began trailing off into those of helpless abandonment. Tired and weak, she wanted to collapse, but instead, she turned and walked slowly to the rock, pathetically leaned her back against it, slid down to the cold, snow-covered ground and wept. She closed her eyes, and tried to pray. She had no prayers, only anguish and gentle weeping, which eventually gave way to gut wrenching sobs.

Shannon felt as if the weight of the world was on her shoulders. She was facing the fact that someday she would have to let Ian go, but she knew it could not be that day. She remained by the cold rock for a few minutes, her crying continuing. She began to pray more fervently than she had ever prayed before, asking God if she had made the biggest mistake in her life. Barely remembering ending her prayers, she walked to the river.

It was a beautiful, sunny, but cold morning. The wind was on her face. She said aloud, "I can see how someone would be tempted to walk into this river to end their anguish." Those thoughts brought her to her senses. In a prayerful statement, she said, "God, I didn't mean that, I would never disgrace you by doing something so horrible. I didn't mean all those mean things I said to you. Please forgive me, but I'm not sure how much longer I can go on. Ian is so fragile. I am so tired and scared. I need to start a business if I am going to survive. I don't know how. I need to love, but I have no one to love. I'm not even sure I still love Ian. I'm just his caregiver." She added, "Please God, have mercy on me. Have mercy on Ian. Please forgive my failings. Please forgive me if I have failed Ian. Please give him back to me, or take us both together." She repeated, "I'm so tired."

Shannon knew she did love Ian. She did not want to live in her wonderful new home without him. She stood there in quiet contemplation. A few minutes later, she asked, "God, if you're still talking to me, will you please tell me something, anything? Thy will be done. Amen."

Shannon realized her arms were raised, as if she were reaching up to the sky. She did not remember raising them. She thought she must have looked like the picture of the girl on the cover of one of the books on her shelf. Again, she fell on the cold bank of the Choptank River, and wept. She wept for herself. She wept for Ian and Michael and for Sean and Kaitlin Rose; they were all entwined in Ian's situation. What would they do if she gave up the house? She wept for the mess she believed she had made of everything. Then she wept for the shame of doubting the God she had worshiped and believed in all her life, the God of her parents. It was her priority prayer. Finally, she headed for home.

As she walked back to the house she thought, "I'm still not sure what I should do, but for today, I will sleep. Tomorrow I will bring Ian home and care for him as long as I have the strength to do so, or until I develop the courage to let him go, so others can care for him." She knew she could not 'put him away' that day. She went back to the house, gave a report of Ian's condition to the couple and went to bed. The next morning she spoke with Doctor Wallace in the hallway outside of Ian's room. She told him of her decision to continue taking care of Ian at home, at least for a while. Doctor Wallace said, "If you really want to take him home, I'll sign the release." He was calming as usual, as he added, "But if you decide you want to consider a care facility, we can keep him for a few days, while you make arrangements. I've compiled a list of ones I would recommend." Shannon nodded and said she would think it over and then let him know later.

She walked into Ian's room, turned on her heels and ran down the hall, yelling, "Doctor Wallace! Doctor Wallace!"

Doctor Wallace, with several personnel following, ran past Shannon, into the room. An excited Shannon cried, "He moved, he moved!" Tears were swelling in her eyes.

After a preliminary examination, Doctor Wallace finally said, "You're right Shannon, there seems to be some activity. Let's watch him and wait awhile."

"Wait?" Shannon muttered. She really wanted to call everyone to come to the hospital, but decided against it, in case it was another false hope. Besides, this was her moment with her Ian. However, she began wondering, "If he awakens, will he know me? Will he know anyone? Will he know anything? Will he be ok? Will he just be a…" Remembering her recent promise to God, she simply said, "Faith."

During evening rounds, the night nurse attached another feeding tube. She had watched Shannon a lot during the previous month and wanted to comfort her, but she remained professional as she left the room, simply saying, "Call me if you need anything." Shannon, knowing the nurse probably repeated the same phrase often, nodded and settled in the chair next to Ian's bed.

In the quiet of the night, she wrote her accounts of the day, closed the journal, deeply inhaled, let out a long tired sigh and closed her eyes. She did not think sleep would come, but needing to rest, her body went to sleep. Her mind did not.

In a dream, Shannon saw a small boy climbing the side of a mountain. Someone was holding his hand, and telling him to keep trying. They needed to get to the top of the mountain. Someone was chasing them. The little boy slipped on small rolling stones. The person who was helping him picked him up, and carried him the rest of the way up to safety.

In another dream, she saw snow. She tried to make a snowman, but the snow quickly changed into rain and completely melted the snowman. As she walked away from her project, the rain changed back to snow. She walked back, gathered snow up in her hands, and began re-making the snowman.

It continued. She finished her project, then she and her newly created, joyful, snowman danced on the snow-covered field.

She opened her eyes. It was morning.

CHAPTER SEVENTEEN
New Morning, New Beginning

Morning,

and with it,
Awareness
Of Dawn, Life, Tranquility, and You...
With me, with me

And from the valley
Of 'Sleep-Won't-Keep'
I awake.

For even in the Valley of Unconsciousness,
I know, I feel, You are near.

With no fanfare, no grand audience, no Christmas Day awakening, no bright shining light overhead, as in the movies,

Ian Ryan Fitzpatrick opened his eyes.
Shannon just stared with hers.

Ian looked over at Shannon and tried to reach out to her, but feeding tubes kept his hands firm. Weak and confused, as anyone coming out of a coma would be, he stared at the several tubes attached to his body. Then he looked over at Shannon.

Shannon had waited and prayed for this moment for more than two years, but seeing Ian looking straight in her eyes actually frightened her. She had her miracle, but sat frozen in shock, temporarily unable to move or speak, barely able to breathe. Her legs were trembling. She clinched the chair arm in the same manner that she had clinched the car door handle, many months ago. When she regained her composure, she pushed the nurse call-button, took a deep breath, forced a smile, and gently touched Ian's hand. Reassuringly, she managed to say, "You're ok."

Soon, Doctor Wallace, two interns and a few nurses were in the room. Shannon stepped just outside the door. The doctor spoke calmly as he approached Ian. Ian seemed frightened.

Shannon happily took a back seat to the activities. She was trembling so severely an orderly had to support her to the waiting room. She was glad for the time to regain her composure. Clenching her fist to steady herself, she vaguely remembered someone bringing her a cold drink and sitting with her.

After a while, she was able to make the exciting call to the cousins, and to Michael. Shortly after that, a nurse came to escort her to Ian's room. His incoherent speech disturbed her. He was very weak, upset and babbling, only able to cry. Shannon sat on the edge of his bed, held him, and allowed him to do so. He was confused and unable to form words. Suddenly, he fell asleep.

Shannon panicked and called for help. The attending nurse assured her that Ian was only sleeping and might do that for days, until his abilities were restored. Shannon took the opportunity to let the cousins know she planned to spend the night at the hospital. She called Michael again, and then rested. She spent the next two days, watching Ian sleep and wake. Each time he awakened, he seemed a little more alert.

Late in the day, on the second day, Shannon awoke in the big easy chair she had use as a bed for more than a month. She realized Ian was staring at her. It startled her. He was finally able to form words. He very pathetically said, "Hi Hon."

She smiled and thought, "Hi, Hon. That's what I get?" She silently repeated, "Hi, Hon?" She wanted to say the phrase aloud, because it was so absurd and almost funny. Instead, she replied, "Hi, yourself, how do you feel?"

Ian weakly answered, "I'm ok, but Shannon, what happened to me. How long have I been in the hospital?"

Shannon, not really lying, answered, "Four weeks." He did not seem to remember the accident. He looked down at the blankets covering his thin body. He could not comprehend the situation. His body was thin; he felt weak. He wondered how he could be in such a weak state in only four weeks.

Ian exclaimed, "Four weeks! I must have been hurt bad. Again, he asked, 'What happened?" Shannon avoided any explanation. She wanted him to remember on his own. Her avoidance of his situation was confusing to him. Suddenly, he cried, "Oh God, I remember…, the truck…the pipes!" In a garbled voice he said, "I remember a truck coming up behind me and a pipe flying past my car." With that recollection, he started to tremble. Shannon put her hand on his hand, to steady him. He asked, "Where was I hurt?"

Shannon, trying to sound calm for fear of sending him into an agitated state, calmly replied to his questions. "You were hurt just about everywhere. I'll tell you more about it later, but you also had a head injury. You've been in a coma." Ian just stared at her, hardly believed what she was saying. Exhausted, he fell asleep. Shannon reminded herself it was normal and tried to relax.

Once, when Ian awoke, he asked, "Is the car OK?"

Shannon started to laugh. It was a nervous laugh to be sure, but a laugh just the same. She answered, "No, the car was totaled."

Ian, struggling to find a voice, again whispered, asking her, "Then, why are you laughing?" Luckily, the doctor entered the room and interrupted their conversation. Ian greeted the stranger, who had been a very important part of his life with, "Hi, Doc."

Even in his weakened state and with a much weaker voice than before, Ian's usual joking manner was charming. Doctor Wallace replied, "Hi yourself, young man. How do you feel?"

Ian answered, "I feel like going home with my wife."

Those words sent shock waves through Shannon. Fear was beginning to surface as she inwardly panicked, "Home? Oh

God, Will he be angry? Will he be able to forgive me?" She prayed, "Oh God, help me."

Doctor Wallace decided Ian should stay in the hospital for a few days to undergo thorough examinations. To Shannon's relief, he suggested she should get a night's rest at home. Ian agreed. She was glad for the time to collect her thoughts and emotions. She also wanted to save Ian's dignity, by giving him a few more days to regain his speech. The doctor promised that no one would tell Ian the truth about his situation. Shannon wanted to break it to him in her own way. She went home. She was secretly glad for the time to think. She checked in with the hospital several times, made some wonderful phone calls, and placed a miraculous based entry in her journal. 'Miraculous' was certainly the operative word.

Intending to give the journal to Ian, she pasted a note on the inside of the last page, with her cell phone number. The message simply stated, "Please, please call me, no matter the hour. I love you very much." She signed it, 'Your Wife.' Before retiring for the night, she called the hospital. A nurse held the phone for Ian. The couple spoke over the phone for the first time since the fateful afternoon of Ian's accident more than two years prior. The voice was certainly different from the saved one on her cell phone, but it was 'her' Ian. All bases being covered, she went to sleep. Blessed, Blessed Sleep!

The next two days were spent with Shannon sitting in Ian's room, waiting for him to return from having various tests. She was glad he slept most of the day when he did return, so she would not have to answer any questions. She did not stay late in the evenings, as she had so often done. She went home to rest before her next hurdle, that of taking Ian to his new home. She knew the next few days would be a time of reckoning with Ian Fitzpatrick. Each night, her last thought before dozing off into dreamland was, "Tomorrow will have to take care of itself."

Early on the third morning, Shannon walked into the hospital room with journal in hand. Ian was out of the room. Glad for the moment to rehearse her speech, she began, "Ian,

I have something to tell you." No, not the right approach. There were no right words. None would suffice. She tried a different approach, "Ian you've been asleep longer than…" Nothing was working.

It was late morning before Ian returned from a final round of tests. Shannon watched him as the nurses helped him back into his bed. Listening to him thanking them, she realized his speech had greatly improved. She thought, "What a beautiful sight." He smiled at her. As frail as he appeared, he was still her Ian. Love was all she felt. OK, love and fear! Fear of disappointing her love.

Ian's voice was sounding stronger and almost normal. As he settled in bed, he asked, "Didja call m'father, Luv?" She loved his thick Irish brogue, and had missed it terribly.

Shannon answered. "Yes, of course, he'll be here tomorrow to take you home."

Ian remarked, "You don't need help taking me home, 'da ya' Luv? Oh, did you tell John and Bea I'm ok?" Without giving Shannon a chance to answer, Ian smiled and went on, "I'm a little weak, but I think I can walk on my own steam and you're a strong one, you are, but I sure want to see m'father, y' know?" Shannon told him, "Yes, I do know and he sure wants to see you too, more than you know!"

As she watched her husband joke with the nurses, Shannon thought to herself, "He's my same old Ian." A thrill came over her. She wished she could enjoy it, but fear replaced the joy. She spent the rest of the morning watching him doze and wake, with him apologizing every time he awoke. After he ate his soft lunch, Shannon spoke. The words almost sticking in her throat, she said, "Ian, Michael will be here tomorrow, but for today I have something for you to read. I could not possibly tell you everything that has happened while you were sleeping, but I've kept a journal of every day's activity since you were hurt. Ian smiled. He knew his wife kept a journal. Sad, angry or glad, she wrote. She asked, "Ian, do you feel strong enough to read?"

Ian answered a strong, "Sure."

Shannon continued, "OK, I'm going to leave you alone for the rest of the day and let you read."

Ian replied, "Sure Hon. By the way, did you call Kim? Will she be over?"

Shannon replied, "Yes, sure I called her. She's thrilled, sends her love and will come to see you soon." Shannon laid the journal on the nightstand, kissed him gently, and went home.

Michael had been a little upset at Shannon's request that he wait a few days before going to the hospital. However, he knew Ian needed medical attention. Shannon needed time alone with Ian, to discuss their new situation, and he, himself, had time to rearrange his work schedule. He had trouble believing Shannon's first phone call. He barely remembered the drive to the hospital.

Shannon had not let Michael speak to Ian, because Ian's speech was upsetting. She hoped it would improve before his arrival.

Michael was shaking as he entered the hospital. He thought, "This is crazy. I washed his wee butt when he was a tyke, and I have been washing his butt these past months, why am I so nervous now? She said he was ok. He's my son, for heaven's sake." He could not believe Ian would was not brain damaged. Shannon could be bracing him for the truth. His fears were dispelled as he walked into the room.

A smiling, but weak Ian asked, "Hi, Dad, you finally decided to get yerself here t'see me?"

Relief was in Michael's smile as he replied, "See ya? I'm going to take the likes of you home where you belong." Remembering the true situation, Michael experienced an immediate rush of adrenaline.

Realizing Michael's dilemma, Shannon told him, "Ian knows everything, Michael."

A weak Ian said, "I read her journal."

Michael, trying to determine Ian's mood, thought he sounded beaten. However, he realized how strange and unsettling everything must be to him. He was not only

148

confused, but was slightly angry. By a twist of fate, he had lost all the control of his life.

Ian knew Shannon was an extremely logical person, a characteristic he loved about her. He knew she did what she had to do to survive, and take care of him. He knew, without her care, he might not have made it. Still, a tiny part of him felt anger, not at Shannon, but at himself. He thought he must have been driving carelessly. He felt inadequate and lost. He wondered if he appeared less of a man in her sight. Would she now regard the likes of him as the weaker one with herself in charge? Confiding in Michael, Ian said after reading Shannon's Journal, his mind was racing all night, and through the morning. He had so many questions:

First: He was in disbelief of the length of time. Was it possible?

Second: Was Shannon angry because he was responsible for her giving up her career?

Third: Will they both be able to continue their careers?

Fourth: Could he have avoided the truck if he had been more attentive? Did he cause the accident because he was speeding, because he promised to get to the Book Signing?

The Book Signing!

Ian's own words triggered a memory. He asked, "Hey, Shannon, how did Matthew's Book Signing go? You never mentioned much of it in your journal, or much about Matthew. Is he a renowned author yet?" Shannon was annoyed at Ian's question, considering what was going on that particular night, and the many days and nights after. She wrote of that night, of continuing days and nights, and her life with Ian, not everyone else's. She was a little hurt by his question, but finally, the irony of his questions took her off guard. She started to laugh. Ian, realizing how odd and out of context the question was, began laughing as well. Michael, relieved at Ian's demeanor, joined in.

Shannon's laughter turned to crying. She was trembling, and almost hysterical. Michael escorted her to the hall, and sat with her until she quieted. Ian was ashamed of hurting her. Shannon had tried to orchestrate everything, to keep a calm atmosphere for Ian, as calm as it could be under the circumstances. She was afraid her crying blew everything. She recovered just in time for Sean and Kaitlin Rose to make their planned appearance.

Michael made introductions, "Ian, meet Kaitlin Rose's new hubby, Sean." Ian shook hands with Sean. With tears in her eyes, Kaitlin Rose gave her cousin a hug and a gentle pat on the shoulder. Ian said he was embarrassed that Kaitlin Rose had been taking care of him, 'ya know'. She did know, but she said it did not matter. She told him it was her profession.

"Oh sure, you get a profession, and use the likes of me for training, huh?" laughed Ian.

"I couldn't ask for a better patient such as yerself," came back Kaitlin Rose. Shannon and Sean could see Ian and Kaitlin Rose were chummy cousins.

The group stayed only a few more minutes. Michael and Shannon promised to arrive early the next morning to take Ian home. Ian was glad for the time alone to gather his thoughts before beginning his new, unfamiliar, journey. In order to stay focused on his predicament, he needed to re-read some of Shannon's journal. As far as he was concerned, he was a hotshot architect one day, and a medical patient the next. There was no twenty-seven months in between, only a day. He felt abnormally weak. Even with the constant therapy, he still needed strengthening.

Early the next day, her dream having come true, Shannon Fitzpatrick walked out of the hospital holding the hand she loved to hold. It was not exactly, as she dreamed. Ian, far too weak to stand on his own and in a wheelchair, never complained as Michael helped him into the backseat of the car. He was more weak and tired than upset, and willingly reclined with Shannon in the backseat. Realizing his dependency, he felt so humble.

With the exception of an occasional sentence, the trip from the hospital was almost a quiet one. The three relatives had their own quiet thoughts.

Michael silently and speaking to his deceased wife, said, "Well Mom, you sure helped me these past months. I could not have kept going if it were not for you. Our boy is alive again. I held him in my very own arms today. I love you, Kaitlin." Then he added, "Please God, continue to watch over our little family." Remembering his and Shannon's first drive down that road, he smiled.

Shannon interrupted Michael's thoughts and prayers, "Looks like a winter wonderland, doesn't it Ian?"

Ian answered with a simple, "Yes it surely does."

Trying to keep the conversation on a happy note, Shannon said, "Holly and Corey are getting married in late September."

Ian answered, "Great, I should be in good shape to travel by then. Are you planning to go?"

Shannon, who had not given any thought to leaving Ian, even for Holly and Corey's wedding, answered, "I would love to, if you're up to it."

"Yep, I will be." Ian answered.

As Shannon watched Ian looking out the window, she thought, "He hates me for bringing him here, I just know it." She wanted to reiterate the message she had written many times in the journal, the message of hope, and if Ian wished, one of returning to the New York, New Jersey area, but his 'Homecoming Day' was not the time to discuss the matter.

As he sat with his head resting on the Shannon's shoulder, Ian could see the sky was a vibrant light blue. The sun was shining. The pure white snow reflected its brightness. The scene appeared to be one of tranquility, but Ian knew his poor Shannon had not felt tranquil while he was sleeping. He watched her looking back and forth between him and Michael, and thought, "She surely has been the victim; I was merely sleeping." His thoughts returned to the first day, in the hospital, when he held her rough worn hands. He thought, "Such hard working, abused, hands. I need to make it up to her."

Thinking of their new home, Ian wondered, "What kind of a house plus three acres could she have possibly purchased for four hundred thousand dollars, and how has she been living?" He also wondered how his cousin from Ireland had been convinced to come all the way to America to take care of him. Sure, he read the journal. Shannon always kept one and always told the truth, but he also knew she loved him. He wondered if she sugarcoated the facts to make him feel better. Had she really believed he would ever awaken? He also wondered if she would be ok going back to New Jersey, and back to work in New York City. By her writings, he knew she had grown to love the area even more than before. The sound of the car's turn signal interrupted everyone's thoughts. Michael maneuvered the car into the driveway just as the mail carrier was driving away, calling out, "Morning, Mrs. Fitzpatrick." Shannon smiled and waved.

Ian, trying to ease the obvious tension with his teasing, said, "Mrs. Fitzpatrick. I love that sound." Michael and Shannon both smiled.

The view from Ian's back seat window was like one he had seen many times in Shannon's winter sketches inserted in the journal. He was looking at the most beautiful white picket fence he had ever seen. It was adorned it with green swags and burgundy bows. Sean had outdone himself. Shannon realized he had added even more touches for Ian. The beautiful fence was in front of a beautiful cottage. Thinking they were stopping at someone else's house, Ian did not prepare to exit the car. The garage door opened. Michael drove the auto into the garage, turned off the engine, got out of the car and walked around the rear passenger side. He opened the door and said, "Welcome home, m' Boy."

Ian was startled. He had expected so much less, but decided to wait to make judgment until after he saw the inside. Already impressed by the beautiful clean spacious garage and then stepping into the 'cottage', he realized it really was not so little. Old Chester had fooled yet another person with his design.

The aromas from the kitchen and fireplace were inviting, but Ian was too exhausted for a tour. Shannon asked if he wanted to rest a while before seeing the rest of the house. He smiled at her, gently touched her face, and said he would like to. He wanted to let her know he was so very appreciative of her efforts to care for him. He fully realized she could have very easily put him in a care facility, just visit him occasionally, and continue in her career. She chose to be hands-on in his care, no matter the pain. As far as he was concerned, that was pure, pure love and devotion.

The 'new' family ate a light lunch. Ian fell asleep on the couch. Michael did the same on the recliner. Shannon was glad for some quiet time alone. She took a brisk walk down the road. She stopped, looked over toward the giant rock and river beyond. She wanted to run to the river, to embrace it and yell to the world, "Ian is alive." She was too tired, and the field was too wet from the melting snow.

Memories of tears, anguish, pain and prayers she had experienced were flooding her mind. She looked up to the sky and meekly said, "Thank you." repeating, "Thank you, God." Tears were running down her cheek. God had answered her prayers. He walked with Ian on his journey back to her. She wrapped her arms around her torso and smiled. She dried her eyes, smiled at the river, turned around, and walked back home to Ian.

Ian felt like a guest in his own home. He seemed uncomfortable. Shannon sadly watched him, hoping he would soon be comfortable with everyone. She also hoped 'their' new home would grow on him as it had on her. After an early dinner, Shannon and Kaitlin Rose cleaned the kitchen. Sean stacked firewood. Ian looked around to the hall leading to the rest of the main floor of the house.

Michael asked, "Ian, are ye' up to seeing the rest of the downstairs now?" Ian nodded. Michael helped him into the wheelchair and took him on a partial tour. He showed him the small rooms and closets on the main floor, and finally, the master bedroom. Sean had offered to take down the two small beds, and replace them with their regular bed, but Shannon wanted to leave everything just as it was. She wanted Ian to see it all for himself. She knew it was important for his psychological healing.

Ian looked at the two beds, and started to weep. Michael closed the door, and let him cry. He asked his father, "Did she grow to hate the likes of me?"

Michael answered, "I've never seen such love flow from anyone in m' life such as from this woman of yours, Ian Fitzpatrick." Then he added, "You've got a lot of making up to do, you know." Ian sadly nodded. They stayed in the room for about a half hour. Sean and Kaitlin Rose were worried. Shannon was not. Ian needed to deal with the reality of the past. She needed to let him. She also felt she did what she needed to do for her sanity and strength as a caregiver. That was that! Period! Ian would have to deal with it.

When the two men finally came out of the bedroom, the hour was late. Ian said he was fine to sleep in the hospital bed for the night. Shannon agreed. She was thrilled just to be able to hear him say, "Good night, Luv."

Everyone seemed to be deep in thoughts, and uneasy in the new situation. Kaitlin Rose interrupted the awkwardness, "I've made Custard. Anyone care for some?"

Sean added, "Ian, you're in for a treat. Kaitlin Rose is the 'Custard Queen."

Actually, Ian had eaten plenty of his cousin's custard back in Ireland, but he went along with Sean's efforts. Trying out his levity, he said, "Well, bring it on!" He knew that the menu, consisting of soft foods, was planned for him. Doctor Wallace had warned him about eating hard to chew, heavy spicy foods.

The fire was warm. The food was wonderful. As late day approached, more timed battery candles lit up the room. The Christmas tree and decorations were still up, adding warmth to the whole winter scene. The outside view was calming. By nightfall, the conversation was lighter. The group was very compatible.

Michael's drive back to Annapolis, three days later, was far better than the ones he had taken over the previous months, but he began wondering if he would lose Ian and Shannon, once Ian totally recovered. His mind wandered to the past autumn, when everyone worked on the 'Farmette', as he teasingly called the home that Shannon had created for everyone. It reminded him of his childhood home, on the family farm in Ireland. He remembered standing on the deck facing the river, praying Ian would someday be able to enjoy the view and all its beauty. God had answered his prayers; his dream had come true.

January 21: The sky had promised, and did deliver, snow, then snow repeatedly. Shannon did not care. She was actually glad. The entire area looked like a winter wonderland. Sean worked outside most days clearing snow and working on projects in the shed and garage. It snowed steadily for one week and off and on for the next, so showing Ian around the property was out of the question.

Sean kept the wrap around deck clear of snow. Ian could go outdoors, and look at the river and property. He could see the field, and off in the distance, the mighty rock Shannon had written about so often in the journal. Shannon was anxious to know Ian's feelings about the place she loved and considered home. However, keeping her thoughts private, she started a new journal. Ian kept her previous one for constant reference.

Ian did a lot of Shannon watching those days as well. She seemed very content, and much stronger than he remembered. Often, his mind wandered back to the journal she so meticulously kept. He knew she did not keep it for any praise for anything she had done or endured. Shannon just always kept a journal. She kept this one especially detailed; praying Ian would someday awaken and be able to read it. Ian was glad she had done so, for he was able to read into her thoughts. He learned of her fears and passions. If he had not already fallen in love with Shannon Marie D'Arcy Fitzpatrick, Ian would surely have through her writings.

Ian often wondered if Shannon actually wanted to go back to work in New York at all. She seemed to fit the house. However, he also wondered if he could continue his career in the new surroundings. Shannon asked him not to worry for the present, rather to concentrate on his nutrition and exercises, to read the newspaper, watch TV, rest and be with her.

The doctor had advised Ian to stay home for two months. Visitations were out. He needed time to heal, and could not risk any contamination. He and Shannon also needed time to heal emotionally. The quarantine allowed Ian time to exercise and become stronger. By the end of two weeks, he was walking on his own, with a walker, but alone just the same. By the third week, he was walking around almost like the old Ian, but with a cane. The fourth week he was walking without a cane, and helping with meals and minor chores.

Each morning Shannon went out to the deck, looked at the snow covered field and the beautiful, snow surrounded river. She thanked God for giving back her Ian, asked for guidance. She thanked Him for the guidance He had given her the past twenty-nine months.

CHAPTER EIGHTEEN
A Valentine Gift

February 14: the day dedicated to lovers. Shannon watched Ian napping by the fire. She thought, "What a wonderful month." Ian was getting stronger each day, and without the burden of stress, so was Shannon. They were not the carefree couple, or passionate lovers they once were, but she was sure, in time, they would be even better. They received many cards and e-mails from well-wishers. A miracle had happened, and all of their friends and families wanted to share in the excitement. Previous cards were very welcome and encouraging. However, Valentines wishes to them, as a couple, were a lot easier to open.

Sean and Kaitlin Rose had planned to make a special dinner for Ian and Shannon, and then retreat to the little cottage for the evening, but Ian and Shannon wanted to do the hosting and invite the cousins to share the evening with them. The cousins gave in.

Sean built a blazing fire in the fireplace. Candles and red and white silk flowers adorned the table. The meal was delicious. After dinner the two couples sat by the fire. The conversation was light. However, Kaitlin Rose seemed distant. Shannon was confused. She and Kaitlin Rose had developed a wonderful sister-like relationship. Actually, she was hurt at Kaitlin Rose's demeanor.

Raising his glass, Ian gave a toast. After taking a tiny sip of wine, Kaitlin Rose jumped up and ran to the bathroom. There she stayed for a few minutes. Shannon's attitude changed from hurt to suspicion. Ian had the same idea. He smiled at Shannon. She smiled back. Sean went in to check on Kaitlin Rose. When they finally returned to the living room, Kaitlin Rose appeared weak. After a few minutes, she ran in again. When she returned to the living room the second time, she was apologetic, and crying. She collapsed in her chair. Getting her a glass of water, Shannon knelt down in front of her, and asked, "Kaitlin Rose, are you pregnant?"

Kaitlin Rose just nodded, and started crying all over again. Shannon asked, "Why are you crying? Aren't you happy about having a little baby?" Kaitlin Rose looked up at Sean, who gave her a sad look. The couple started to speak at the same time and then paused.

Finally, Sean simply said, "Yes and no."

Ian asked, "Why would ye say no, Sean?" Suddenly Ian knew why. They were worried about having a place to live should he and Shannon decide to move. One of them needed employment and a sponsor in order to stay in the America. He realized that Kaitlin Rose and Sean were worried that the insurance would no longer be paying for Kaitlin Rose's nursing.

"Maybe, neither Sean and nor m' own self will be needed any longer. I'll be of no use to anyone in this condition. We're not supposed to start our family yet. We are not ready. I don't know how this happened."

Ian put his hand out to shake the hand of the shaky expected father. He laughed and said, "I do."

Shannon put her arms around Kaitlin Rose and said, "Kaitlin Rose, you and Sean are our family. This is more than exciting news. It is another miracle! You have three people here to take care of you. You have done so much for us. Now it is our turn. You will be included in any decisions we make. Sean can finish school, and find employment, if you wish to stay in America." With a twinkle in her eyes, she added, "Besides, do you remember our own Irish Ambassador? Now, are you ok?"

"I'm ok," answered the exhausted Irish girl. She handed Sean her glass of wine. It turned out to be a more wonderful Valentine's Day than anyone could have imagined.

Shannon and Kaitlin Rose spent the next few days excitedly talking about baby things, making appointments, discussing nursery furniture, boy/girl colors, asking and answering questions: Would the couple like to have the upstairs bedroom permanently, and the adjoining tiny room turned into a nursery? They made phone calls, many phone calls. The grandmums from Ireland were already planning their visit to Maryland.

With Ian very much awake, and a baby joining the family, Shannon knew God had given her a new life. She, occasionally, awoke to check on Ian, to be happily reminded that he was peacefully sleeping next to her in 'their' bed. She would think of the little one who would soon join their family. When the realization, that she was actually thinking 'baby' and 'family', would sink in her brain, she would sigh, and whisper, "A baby! What a wonderful life." Then she would gently drift off to sleep. Ian would smile and pull her close.

Several of their neighbors, after hearing of Ian's recovery, had already stopped by only long enough to drop off get-well gifts of pies, cakes, homemade candies, etc. Nurse Kaitlin Rose actually cleaned the food containers with sanitizing wipes before bringing them into the kitchen. Their friends knew visits would be very welcome later. Michael, taking every precaution, got preventative shots and wore only freshly dry-cleaned, or laundered clothing. He came every weekend during the first few weeks of Ian's recovery, assuring Shannon he would not be such a pest once Ian was 'up and running' as he put it. He told Ian and Shannon he would pay Sean's salary if they wanted to keep him on for at least a year while Ian re-established his architectural career.

While his motive may have been selfish in the hopes of keeping his children in the area for at least a year, Michael was solving a few problems. One weekend when he was visiting, he said to Ian, "This area could certainly use a good architect. Lots of construction going on, down in Ocean City." Shannon knew he was doing a selling job. However, she had decided that Ian would make the final decision regarding their home location. She made the previous one. Ian deserved the right of choice. She held her breath a lot.

Ian spent many moments alone, walking around the deck, looking over the property and especially, the river. It did seem mystical. He felt as if he knew the place even without a tour. He knew Chester, who phoned often to check on him. He knew Bill and Pat, and Bill's mom, Ruthie, and he knew Martha's family. He knew everyone and everything through Shannon's journal. He read it, day after day, night after night, hardly believing all that had taken place. He grew more deeply in love with the woman he married. He knew her strength, her weaknesses and soul. The more he read, the more he loved her. He even grew to know and love the 'Spirit' and did believe it once existed, if only in Shannon's imagination.

One bright morning during the first week of March, Ian stood leaning on the back deck banister, looking over at the field, the river and the 'rock'. He remembered Shannon's sad experience when they were traveling in the area, and then later at the motel. He remembered the panic in her voice. He whispered, "My God! It was so real to her." He actually became emotional when he thought of her going through the experience alone.

CHAPTER NINETEEN
Kim Re-Visits the River

Mid-March: Ian and Shannon had their first outing. Ian spent two days in the hospital for a thorough physical. Doctor Wallace declared him to be in tip-top condition. Shannon already knew that. To celebrate, they stayed at the Inn where Shannon and Michael had eaten their first meal in the area. During dinner, Ian touched Shannon's wine glass with his, and said, "I love you more today than I ever have, Shannon Marie D'Arcy Fitzpatrick." He caressed her face the way he used to. Shannon almost had to pinch herself to believe he was real. By morning, she had no doubt.

The drive back to the river was almost as romantic as their last vacation. It was a wonderful day. However, Shannon was distracted by wondering if she could be just as happy if Ian wanted to move back up north. She silently reminded herself that she already decided he could choose where they would live; tomorrow would have to take care of itself. She smiled and enjoyed the ride home.

One year after Kim's first visit and during the second week of March, Kim, Keith and Keith's mom, Kathryn, paid a visit to the Choptank.

Michael also came for the weekend. Although Kim had been speaking to Ian over the phone, very often since his recovery, she still could not believe he was completely healed. Their visit was special. Kim was excited to see Ian and to introduce him to her new husband. Ian was nervous meeting Keith, knowing they had certainly met under the most unusual circumstances. Keith was concerned for Ian's embarrassment, but he was happy, for there would be a voice to the body, he had help nurse. Shannon actually felt threatened. She feared the conversation would lead to the theater. Kim, now having Shannon's job, could possibly want to give it back. It was odd. Just a few years prior, Shannon was praying to get such a job, but the day of Kim's visit, she was praying Kim would not offer it back to her. She did not want Ian to have a reason to 'give back' her career. She was happier in her new surroundings than she ever imagined she could be. She wanted to fish and garden, to can and freeze her harvest, and to cook and bake. She wanted to live with Ian on the Choptank River and she wanted to paint. She especially wanted to help raise the little one who was on its way to their home. She also hoped to raise a family of her own. In her new peaceful state, she could dream again. Remembering her (and Ian's) promise to Sean and Kaitlin Rose, she wondered if they would be happy living up north if it came to that.

Kim noticed her friend's anxiety right away, and kept the conversation strictly on Ian, and the great way he looked. She bragged about the way Shannon had taken to 'Southern Living' etc. etc. etc. To Shannon's delight, Kim kept her part of the conversation strictly on their adventures and the delight of Ian's recovery.

Michael was happy to see Kim and Keith, and especially pleased that someone of his generation had joined them for the weekend. Michael and Kathryn seem to hit it off. Shannon watched Kim smile at the older couple who were walking down by the river. She thought, "Hmm, wonder if some match-making is going on?"

Ian shared the same theory with Shannon later, when they were alone. He missed his mom, but loved the way his father's face lit up when he first met Kathryn. He also shared his feeling that the life they had lived and loved, seemed so far away, and so long ago. She wondered just how he meant that statement. Identifying his moods was difficult.

The visit from Kim's family was brief, but good. They left early on Monday morning, accepting Ian and Shannon's invitation to spend their summer vacation on the river. Kathryn was included in the invitation. Ian and Shannon suspected Michael would be seeing her before then.

CHAPTER TWENTY
The Walk

On a mild late-March afternoon, the sun was shining. The snow had melted, and it was a surprisingly warm day. Ian, well acquainted with the immediate property, wanted to see the rest of it. He and Shannon took a walk. Coming to a bend in the road, he joked, "I remember this place. This is where you almost beat me up when I wouldn't stop the car."

Trying to make light of Ian's frivolity, Shannon smiled, and simply replied, "Yes it is."

They walked a little further. When he realized how far they had walked, Ian asked, "Is this still our property?"

Shannon, not sure if he was impressed or concerned, answered him, "Yes, the acre and half the house and buildings are on, half-acre on the west side and two to the east."

Ian teased, "You are some negotiator, Shannon Fitzpatrick. I absolutely cannot believe you purchased all of this for four hundred thousand dollars, and the man still comes around and works on the property." Shannon smiled. She and Chester Fargo shared a special love no one would understand. They both loved Arlene's paradise, had a love for the Choptank River, a love for the Chesapeake Bay, and a very special understanding of the love they each had for their spouses.

The bus shelter provided a resting place. Ian put his hands behind his head and looked up to the sky in contemplation. Shannon kept quiet. She knew the feeling. He needed to take in the wonder of the day. Watching his wife caress the bench, he said, "Nice little cover for the kids."

Shannon answered, "Yes it is. Bill's father built it." Ian smiled. Shannon seemed to caress everything she encountered in their new home: the bench, the table, the railing on the deck, even the garage wall. He remembered an entry in the journal, one that he read many times:

"I walked into the garage today and wondered how many times the old couple must have walked through this very garage to go shopping, to visit the kids, or to go to a movie? I could not keep from touching the clean wall. He built this house with his own hands for her. No garage is ever this clean. I love the way he looks and sounds when he speaks of her. He must have loved her very much and she loved him back. I hope Ian will love me like that when we're old."

Reading the passage aloud to Shannon one night, Ian whispered to her, "I do, and I will."

As they walked home, Shannon looked longingly at the big rock. She almost missed the feeling of familiarity. The feeling was gone, and so she reasoned the 'Spirit' must be at peace. She took some satisfaction in the knowledge that, if there actually had been an unhappy spirit among them, there is also a possibility of her own prayers, somehow, helping it find peace. She said nothing, nor did Ian. The words in her journal sufficed. First was the fear, the mystery, the anguish and then, the love. Ian knew she would verbally share it with him when she was ready. That day, she was not. She had actually shared so much with him through her written words. Conversation about it was not necessary. Ian understood. He decided if she ever wanted to talk about it, they would. He would wait.

Ian began to weaken. Shannon offered to call Sean. He refused. Slowly, he managed to continue on his own. They stepped upon the deck, walked around to the riverside, and leaned against the railing facing the water. Ian looked down at the river, then eastward to the little cottage. He smiled gently, knowing Chester spent many happy hours there as he planned, and created his paradise.

Ian looked even farther eastward toward the field, the rock and beyond. Pointing to the field with the giant rock, he said, "That spot would be an awesome place for our dream house. The towering rock could be like a giant bird, a landmark for our water-traveling visitors. We could build a handsome dock by it, a giant wing dock." He smiled at his own architectural cleverness.

Shannon's heart jumped with joy. She actually held her breath for an instant for fear of interrupting Ian's words with her own excitement. She did not want to break the spell. In an immediate silent prayer she thought, "He wants to stay! He wants to stay! Thank you God! Thank you!" She had to agree about the other field, and was content about the rock being a part of her future home, still, she felt hurt that he did not like the house that she now called home. Sounding very hurt, she asked, "Ian, do you not like this house?"

Ian answered, "Oh sure, who wouldn't like this house. I grew to love it through the passion in your journal. It is a wonderful house. It is a dream all right. However, it was Chester and Arlene's dream. Our investments have produced. You have managed our money well. You have even added income to it. We will be getting a large settlement from the trucking company. Now I want, more than ever, to build the house of our dream. We should build it here, together, Ok?"

That made sense. Shannon was thrilled at the magic word, 'Here.' She was thrilled he wanted to stay on the river. However, she wondered about their house. She could not bear to sell it and certainly would not just abandon it. It was never Ian's intention to do either. He took his wife's hand, and led her down the steps to the river. They stood on the pier, and looked over the water. The March winds were beginning to dominate the treetops. The water was churning and beating against the rocks. Still, they felt warmth from the sun.

Ian said, "I noticed there was more field beyond our property, maybe we could purchase it, add to ours, and maybe build a stable." He smiled as he looked over again at the little studio cottage and continued, "The cottage is cute and warm enough. Sean and Kaitlin Rose are satisfied to have it for their temporary home, but wouldn't it be great to have them and their wee one as neighbors, if they decided to stay in America?"

Shannon said nothing, just smiled, turned and looked at the cottage, and then back to him. She knew they were home.

The three o'clock sun shining across Ian's shoulders blinded her. Standing in his shadows, she could barely see him, but felt his presence near her, beside her, in front of her, surrounding and overwhelming her. She was thrilled to be his life partner, thrilled to be able to think those thoughts again and thrilled to be able to continue their dream. She looked up to the blinding sky and said aloud, "Thank you God. Thank you. Thank you for Sean, Kaitlin Rose and the baby. Thank you for Michael. Thank you for everyone. Thank you for bringing Ian back to me." She looked lovingly toward the field, the rock, and at the beach in front of it. She added, "And thank you God, for blessing my friend." Ian smiled at her words.

A breeze moved Shannon's hair. She felt compelled to turn and look toward the field and rock, and then beyond, to the bend of the river. She felt a gentleness, as if someone were laying praying hands on her. Ian smiled, knowing she was at peace. She looked up at him. He looked into her eyes as if seeing them for the first time. Securing her in his arms, he kissed her tenderly, and then released his hold on her. He lovingly rested his arm around her shoulders. She placed her hand over his. As they stepped onto the deck, he looked in at the cozy living room beyond the French doors; happy that Shannon brought him to their cottage, and now she knew it. Looking in on the warm scene, he teasingly said, "You never bought any new furniture."

Shannon kept walking as she simply asked, "Do I have to do everything?"

They walked into their home.

CHAPTER TWENTY-ONE
A Farewell Prayer

S haahatuck stood on the warm, wet, spring sand, looking up river.

Smiling tenderly, she, appreciatively, looked at Shannon, remembering the times they grieved their lost loves by the Prayer Rock.

She also remembered the prayers Shannon voiced for her.

She remembered the release of her 'self-inflicted 'bond of guilt, being lifted by Shannon's prayers.

She also remembered their collective tears that bathed the Prayer Rock.

She was sorry Shannon probably did not know the depth of love and gratitude she felt for her.

She looked over the river, raised her right hand gently as if to bless it, and then, keeping her hand in a prayer position, looked to the young couple.

She especially, smiled at her friend, Shannon.

She prayed,

"My Dear Friend,

"My river I leave to you. Love it dearly. Use it wisely.
"Cherish its beauty. Enjoy its bounty.

Raise your little ones on its sacred banks. Let them gather its precious stones, and play on its golden shores,

"But jealously guard those little ones, for my river is deep, and it will beckon them to come into its refreshing water.

"My River will give you love, and swell your soul. It will wash your face with its refreshing mist.

"It will calm your spirit by its awesome grace, and let you hear the beautiful voice of the Father Spirit in the Clouds,

"But, it will also take you away with its rushing waters, devour your body with its violent storms, and bury you deep in its soggy bowels.

"All these are a part of my Choptank, my home I leave to you. I thought I would miss it, but I now go to a better place, and I have you to thank.

"You believed in me, when others would not. Others felt my pain, but ran away.

You felt my pain and knew I was real.

"You followed me to my river.
You love it as I do.
You showed me love.

"You prayed for me and shared my tears.
"Now I give love back to you.

"*The Father Spirit* allowed *me to come to you for a precious moment, to pray for you. May He smile upon you, and give you many little ones, and many years of love with your own brave.*

"May you always love as you love today.

And

"When you come home to live with the Father Spirit,

"I will embrace you…my 'Sister."

The Author

Interview by Keith Ketterer

Yvonne Dorsey

"I was born on the top of a mountain simply called, "Big Mountain" near Quinwood, West Virginia. Dad had eight siblings. Mom had twelve. My two brothers, Chuck and Wally, were also born on the mountain. We lived there until a coal company hired Dad in the capacity of a miner.

We moved into company housing, called a "Coal Camp House" in Bellburn, West Virginia, another smaller mountain near the coal mine where Dad worked. Youngest sibling, Rose was born in the coal camp.

"Coal Camp Houses were provided for rent to coal miners and their families only as long as the miner was employed at the mine. The families usually made their purchases at the Company Store, which sold various items like food, work boots, shovels, blankets, pillows, furniture, Christmas decorations, appliances and more. The items were listed on the miner's account. The rent, plus monies owed for items purchased, was deducted from the miner's earnings, before he received his pay.

"In our case, church services were held on the second floor of the Company Store. Mom played the organ. Dad taught Sunday School. We also attended the Mt. Zion Methodist Church that Dad help build, on Big Mountain. It is still a tiny, beautiful, wonderful place our family visits when we are in West Virginia.

"World War II was in progress when we lived in the Coal Camp. Dad was rejected for military service because he was missing two fingers on one hand, a result of a mining accident. However, he did find a way to serve his country. He collected tin cans from neighbors and flattened them. Every Saturday, he loaded the tin in his car. He delivered his carload to the government collection site at the train depot, to be used for the war effort.

"On occasion, at night, a loud siren would blow, announcing a Blackout Drill. Everyone had to turn off all lights as a practice of security in the event of an enemy attack by air.

"During the drills, we children were afraid, so Dad would play the guitar to calm us. We sang. It was soon over, and the lights were turned back on. Luckily, we never had to hear the real siren.

"My brothers and I spent many cold weather afternoons and evenings sitting, and playing, in front of the fireplace. One afternoon, Dad came home, and stood smiling at my brothers and me. Suddenly, we heard a little cry coming from his big pocket. He pulled out a little black and white puppy. He said we could name it. We called him Poochie.

"Poochie quickly elected his favorite person…Dad, escorting him to the end of the camp each morning when Dad walked to meet the other miners, then came home for his breakfast. When the three o'clock whistle blew, he knew Dad would be returning from the mines. He returned to the entrance of the camp and accompanied Dad home.

"One August day, Dad was killed in the coal mines. Poochie still awoke early to walk Dad to the edge of the camp. After a long while, he would go to sleep, and sleep most of the day. Each afternoon, he walked to the end of the camp when he heard the three o'clock whistle. He waited until dark, until he finally gave up and returned home. He did that for weeks, until he became ill.

We moved Poochie to my aunt's (one of Mom's eight sisters) farm, because we needed to vacate our home, and could not take him with us. Only miners' families could rent the houses and our miner was dead.

"Our family of six was then, a family of five. Our Mom, who had never had a paying job, had to find work. She also had never driven a car, so we had to live close to wherever she could find work.

"Our first big move was during World War II. After struggling to support her family in West Virginia, Mom secured employment in a factory in New Jersey. We lived with an aunt, (another one of her eight sisters), whose husband was serving in the war. I was in the first grade in school, and very afraid of, what I thought were aggressive, 'Yankee' children.

"When the war was officially over, my uncle had fulfilled his tour of duty and was returning home. We had to move out of our aunt's apartment. Our grandfather, who had assumed authority, but gave no financial aid, over my mom's family, suggested that we moved back to West Virginia, to my aunt's farm. By that time, our aunt, pregnant with her fifth child, was also a recent coal miner's widow. We followed his advice. When we arrived, Poochie was there waiting for us.

"The two sisters had nine children between them. They established a good working relationship, and with the help of their children, worked the farm. This arrangement worked nicely for a while, until the two women needed to find their own happiness. They went their separate ways, but remained close sisters.

"We remained in West Virginia until I graduated eighth grade, when we moved back to New Jersey, where work for Mom was more profitable. Our aunt in West Virginia agreed to keep Poochie. He loved the farm, and lived there until his death.

"In New Jersey, Mom began driving a car. We established

ourselves in schools and work, developed families and, as families do, scattered countrywide, but have maintained a close family relationship.

"I have lived, and worked in several states, and enjoyed all of them. I especially loved the years I spent in the Chesapeake Bay area in Maryland, and still travel there to visit some of my family.

"I currently live in historic Clinton, New Jersey, a small town graced with a river running through it, complete with a grist mill and waterfall, providing camera bugs with a picturesque subject, and fishermen with a bucket of trout. I attend the Clinton United Methodist Church, and enjoy socializing with good friends. I have three grown children and three grown grandchildren.

"In 1988, four days after her birthday, Mom died at the young age of sixty-nine. Dad's last suit was found wrapped in tissue paper and placed in a bottom dresser drawer. Even through all of her moves, she kept it near her. She must have loved him very much. I think of them often. Much of their life, and my memories, are reflected in my writings. I dedicate all works to their loving memory.

30010403R00110

Made in the USA
Middletown, DE
10 March 2016